AF585636

The Reverter

by

Achintya Nigam

This novel is entirely a work of fiction. The names, characters and incidents portrayed in it are the product of the author's imagination. Any resemblance to actual persons, living or dead, or events or localities is entirely coincidental.

Paperback Edition 2024

ISBN: 978-93-340-9144-1

Copyright © ACHINTYA NIGAM/2024

ACHINTYA NIGAM asserts the moral right to be identified as the author of this work. All rights reserved in all media. No part of this publication may be reproduced, stored in a retrieval system, or transmitted, in any form, or by any means, electronic, mechanical, photocopying, recording or otherwise, without the prior written permission of the author and/or publisher.

The Reverter

by

Achintya Nigam

Science Fiction

CONTENTS

Earth Births A Sun

I

"Finally! Let's eat!" My roommate opened the box and carefully served the rice onto the plates.

"So, Anirudh, how was your day?" Sarvesh asked me.

"The usual, finish the entries, get yelled at by your boss for misplacing a date, and sit for extra hours to get it fixed."

"Well, that's awful."

"Yeah, I just wish I could return to how things were during high school."

"Me too, the war…it played a game with our lives."

"The war..." I stared at a grain of rice on my plate. Tiny and delicate, it resembled our current world.

"Here, have some of the paneer," Sarvesh said, pouring the cottage cheese and gravy over the rice. The soft rice was now drenched in a red liquid, which made me feel rather nauseous.

The things that this war had shown us: the deafening screams of the children, mothers wailing with their sons and daughters all but alive in their hands, the vast emptiness in the soldiers' eyes. And all because a few politicians couldn't keep their egos inside their pockets…well it was more complicated than just that, but yes, they could have handled it much more peaceful.

"I am sorry...I can't eat right now," I unmistakingly uttered.

Sarvesh looked at me with saddened eyes, as he momentarily stopped eating. The spoon dropped with a loud clank onto the plate.

"Shouldn't have brought up the war. No worries, you can have it in the morning. Go get some rest, you've had a long day," he said as he began eating again and tried not to make eye contact with me.

I got up and went to my room.

Lying on my bed, I thought: Why couldn't everything be normal? Why is it that every day we must hear about the fatalities of this ludicrous war? I wished I could go back to the old days. Back when all everyone cared about was scoring marks on their tests. But here we were, living in the fear that each breath we take could be our last. The doomsday clock had struck 1 second to midnight and was inching ever closer.

My eyes were starting to get heavy and sooner than I knew, I had fallen asleep.

"You know you're going to fail," my invigilating teacher said to me glaring down disdainfully at my blank test paper.
Following that comment, the whole class erupted in laughter. Staring at me, not pointing fingers, but just laughing maniacally.

I tried to focus on my paper but was interrupted by a girl who patted my back.
The teacher had disappeared, so I looked back and realised it was my high school crush.
She had short, bouncy hair and wore tiny round earrings. She had this smile that always made my heart melt away. Her eyes were like black diamonds in a sea of pearly-white clouds, and her distinct and subtle brown complexion soothed my eyes.
I wished she worked in the same office as me. Which made me think: what was I doing in my high school anyway?

I have tons of work to finish. I can't waste my time on some lousy test!

She was about to say something; her mouth puckered. But everything had slowed down. It was as if I could feel the weight of the world on me. And as if the weight of the world was too much, everything started to shake. I looked at her and she looked at me.

But before I could say anything, I woke up. My roommate screamed, "Anirudh! We need to go!" Pulling at me with his full strength.

As I got back to my senses and looked out the window, my heart pounded loudly, my eyes wide with fear. I couldn't hear my roommate screaming anymore. It was as if someone had taken my ears out and dumped them in a swimming pool. But I could see. Outside was a horrifying mushroom cloud, as bright as the sun, slowly expanding upwards in the distance.

The sound of the sirens slowly started fading in, as did my roommate's shrieks. He had finally pulled me out of the bed and out of the room.

"Sarvesh! What is happening?"

"I got a notification saying that Mumbai has been attacked! They are evacuating everyone out of Pune!"

"Wait!" I screamed at Sarvesh. He stopped and let go of me.

"I need to get my passport!"

"No! we need to go!"

"Just wait for a second!" I yelled while running to my room to get my wallet, passport, phone, and aadhar card. I emptied my laptop bag, stuffed everything inside, and ran out of my room, dashing towards the front door of the apartment.

"When did this happen?" I asked.

"I am not sure! I just woke up and saw the message on my phone!"

"Damn!"

We almost flew down the stairs, and although it looked like the shock wave from the blast would be coming soon, it was at least ten minutes away (according to the government warning notification on my phone at least).

We reached the ground floor in under five minutes.

And there it was, 7 minutes early.

The shock wave.

We were now lying flat on the ground. My ears were ringing, and I could feel a sharp pain in my chest. My shirt had been rip ped and there were huge scratches all over my chest. Although I was wearing shorts, my legs were unscathed.

Probably because my chest took most of the fall damage.

I slowly got up. The ringing in my ears had stopped. I could see some trees uprooted. But before I could notice anything else, I saw Sarvesh lying down.

"We...need..to..go..." Sarvesh called to me, in a very weak voice. Thank God he was alive.

"Oh my God! Sarvesh, are you ok?", I rushed to him. I put one of his arms on my shoulder and grabbed him.

"I think...I think I've sprained my ankle"

"Shit! Don't worry, I got you. Let's get out of here."

We tried to head towards the main street as fast as we could with Sarvesh injured.

There were glass pieces everywhere. And chaos seemed to reign supreme. People were screaming and running. Families getting in their cars, hurrying to leave. Some people took advantage of the chaos and looted the nearby stores. They were probably looking for food, water, and other resources, which could be scarce now. It was also very dark, no street lights were on.

A policeman, shouted on a megaphone, "Citizens, please head to the evacuation vehicles immediately!" A little further ahead, I could see the buses ready to depart.

"There's the bus! We can leave! I am sure there will be someone at the bunker to help you with your leg!" I told Sarvesh, but he was not paying much attention. Maybe he didn't hear me because of the noise.

But he looked at me, then towards the buses without saying a word. I couldn't understand what he was going through, but it seemed that he was disconnecting himself from the world.

I stared at the mushroom cloud. It was now as tall as Mount Everest, maybe even taller. Although we were in Pune (a city 150kms away from Mumbai) we were far from safe.

We soon got on the bus, and it left after a minute.

I didn't think a nuclear strike was possible. Sure, the doomsday clock had struck 1 second to midnight, but I didn't think the world leaders would launch the missiles for real.

However, they did.

But was it only Mumbai that was attacked, or was it all around the globe? I checked my phone, and it was surprisingly still getting a signal. So I decided to check the news.

My heart sank; my hands shook. It was not just Mumbai that was attacked...

BEEP! BEEP!

My phone buzzed and beeped, and so did everyone else's

"RED ALERT MISSILE DETECTED. ESTIMATED STRIKE: AREA 100 KM RADIUS CONCERNING YOUR CURRENT LOCATION. EVACUATE TO THE NEAREST BUNKER IMMEDIATELY ETA 7 MINUTES."

The message repeated itself several times after going back to normal.

I looked at Sarvesh. He looked back at me and then turned to face the window. "I am going to sleep," he said, "don't wake me up." Sarvesh had lost a lot in the war, his family, his job, his home, and finally…himself. He just wanted to forget everything that was happening and sleep it all away. And I couldn't blame him for doing so.

I now had also lost my family.

I opened my backpack and took out my wallet. Inside was a photograph of me and my parents. I stared at it and smiled while tears flowed down my face. They couldn't have survived the blast in Mumbai.

We knew what was coming. We knew this could happen. Yet we remained silent. If given a second chance, I would do anything I could to stop this from happening.

God, I just wanted to go to the past and relive my life again.

"5 MINUTES TO STRIKE. SEEK BUNKER IMMEDIATELY," the alarm blared again.

There was a couple in the front seat and the woman had a toddler with her. He started crying from the incessant beeps of the alarm system. The mother's efforts to calm down the child were in vain.

The father suddenly stood up.

"Driver!" He shouted with his voice trembling, "Can't you take us to a shelter?"

"The nearest shelter is at least half an hour away."

And with that, the father sat back in his seat and covered his face with his hands.

The child hadn't stopped crying.

I put my wallet back in my bag. I had thrown my phone inside the bag before bringing out the wallet, so I searched for it. But instead, I found something squishy.

I took it out and realised that it was a packet of candies.

The child was still crying. Maybe I should give him these candies? I stood up and went to the front seat. Then I got down on my knees and gave the child the candies. He magically stopped crying and started looking at the packet with great interest. Turning it around, up and down, he seemed satisfied with it. His mother then opened the packet and his eyes widened. She took one of the jelly-like beans and placed it in his mouth. It filled the child with delight.

The mother looked at me with watery eyes and mouthed, "Thank you." I smiled at her and slowly went back to my seat.

"STRIKE IMMINENT! TAKE SHELTER IMMEDIATELY!" said the unhelpful AI.

Someone smashed their phone on the bus wall. I could understand his frustration.

Sarvesh had fallen asleep even with such noise. He looked at peace.

I looked ahead. A herd of cars and buses moved ahead. A traffic jam was taking place. we wouldn't reach anywhere before the strike.

These seven minutes felt like an hour now. Any second could be our last. The alarm had stopped showing an ETA. Moments from my whole life started popping in front of me. My brain knew that I was about to die and as if to comfort me, it showed me the best memories I had made in this insignificant life of mine.

And soon, there it was.

Right in front of my eyes.

The road, once black, was now red. It was the birth of another sun. A new sun right here on Earth.

I could feel the heat of the surroundings increasing.

I slowly closed my eyes and wished I could go back to my high school days. I prayed that someone would listen and save us from this misery. I prayed that someone would hit the undo button and revert this godforsaken world to peaceful times.

But nothing...

The heat was still increasing; it felt like someone was piercing my skin with needles. My eyes were bright, even though I had closed my eyes. I couldn't bear this anymore. The pain had become unbearable, but there was no air for me to scream with. And then—silence. Everything was suddenly dark and calm.

I could no longer feel any pain. Maybe I was in heaven? I felt nothing, not even my weight. It was as if someone had dropped me off an aeroplane. I didn't feel scared; it was all just serenity and silence. I had never felt so at peace before.

Slowly, I felt the weight of my body and the sound in my ears returning. At first, I could hear the wind, then some birds, some people talking, and some low rumbling noises, the same kind you would have noticed if you lived in a city. I could feel my feet, and I could feel a solid surface beneath them.

I slowly opened my eyes. I was expecting myself to be in some sort of cloud, but instead, I was in a room that looked oddly familiar.

"Anirudh! It's 5 already! I know the tuition classes are just 5 minutes away, but you should reach early!"

I turned around to see my mother staring at me.

"What? Get your bag, and leave!" she screamed.

"What? How? What is this!? Why...why am I in my old house?" These were the thoughts that raced through my head.

2019

II

"Hey, are you ok? You look very stressed."
I sat down on the bed to my right.

My mother came and sat beside me and ran her fingers through my hair comfortingly. I was confused, but I had to say something to her.
"I...I have a headache"

She then put her hand on my forehead and said, "You don't seem to have a fever...but...look, if something is wrong, you can tell me. The Annu I know won't let a simple headache stop him." She smiled at me, her eyes glistening with love for me.
"Oh...I know what's wrong! You forgot to do your homework!"
"Yeah..."
"Oh, don't worry! I will talk to your teacher. Besides, he will be angrier if you're late."
She kissed my forehead and then left my room.

I looked around the room. This was my room from when I was in school, and that woman was my mother. But how was this possible? What was happening?

I found a bag on my study table in front of me. I stood up and looked at the bag. It was my tuition bag. And beside it was my phone (my old phone). It was a metallic blue, Samsung Galaxy A7. It had what appeared to be 2 camera lenses in the back. I received this phone as a birthday gift when I was in my 9th std. Later on, as I started my job, I changed it to a cheaper Nokia G42.

I slowly went to the table and picked it up, pushing the power button at the same time. I couldn't believe it.

The lock screen read: 5:02 5th April 2019.

"Wait, this means that I am at the beginning of my tenth standard!" I shouted in disbelief.

Maybe a little too loud.

"What was that Annu?"

"Nothing...it turns out I finished my homework!"

"Then leave already!"

"Yes, Ma!"

The weight of the phone felt unfamiliar. I mean, of course, it did! But I couldn't understand how my hands felt so thin. I kept the phone back and started looking at my hands

I then felt my face and had an immediate urge to look in the mirror. I quickly went to my mother's dressing table and looked at my body at full length.

My eyes were wide as I stared at myself; A 15-year-old boy in fresh clothes. Clothes that I am sure had long since been thrown away. But here I was wearing them.

So, I had somehow travelled to the past? My head spun. How was this possible? A few minutes ago, I was in the middle of a nuclear blast, and now I was here? How was any of this possible?

I looked around the room I was in, my parents' bed-room. It was exactly like I remembered.

I went back to my room while carefully studying the hallway as if looking for changes, or irregularities, if any. But no, the tiled walls with reflective marble, the small bulb light at the top, which I had to change multiple times in the past…it was exactly like in my memories. I looked at my room.

Nothing had changed. It was all the same.

I put on my bag and sandals. If I was really in 2019, I needed to see the world to confirm it.

Not that my current house was any less of an indicator, but my mother probably wouldn't stop nagging me unless I left. So, I decided to head out.

I moved towards the lift, pressed the button, and the door opened. I got in the lift, and while it went down, I contemplated the possibilities about what exactly was happening.

Was I in heaven? Maybe. Is this one of those experiences in which people see their entire lives right before they are going to die? But I was already dead, right? The blast should have killed me instantly. Is this what happens in the afterlife? Do you randomly go back to some time in your past? The last theory seemed the most plausible. But was it?

The lift door opened.

"Ground floor," a female robotic voice iterated.

I headed out. This was the main lobby of my building. Everything was exactly as I remembered. I spent nine years here. The white marble floors and the walls of the lobby were painted golden yellow, the nameplates of the residents, which always had dust on them, and the CFL bulbs that lit up the lobby, looked exactly the same.

Out of the lobby, there was the main gate of the building. The watchman at the gate looked at me as I went out the gate and then went back to listening to the radio on his phone. The neighbouring buildings and housing societies all looked exactly like I remembered.

The cars parked on the side of the road reminded me of the time me and my friends had broken a window of one car, and how the car owner had castigated us for it.

I walked onto the road leading to my tuition classes and headed towards the gate of the tuition building. But as I reached the gate of the building, I stopped. I couldn't believe it. My eyes became teary. In front of me was my best friend, Rohit Srivastava. At the start of World War 3, Rohit had lost his family to a bombing while he was studying in Berkeley. So he came back to India and joined the army. He died fighting in the war in 2024.
I ran towards him. He was alive!
"Hey, Anirudh! I was just about to call you!"

And then I grabbed his shoulders. It was seeing him that I realised that the reason I wanted to go back to my high school days was because I missed everyone. I missed my mother, my father, him, and so many more people...maybe this was God's gift to me. I had prayed about this so much, and I was being given what I wanted! Or I hoped this was what had happened. Now I could spend more time with everyone. Do things that I regretted not doing and abstain from those that I regretted.

"Hey...you ok?", I also realised that I had been staring at him for 30 seconds straight with my hands on his shoulders. I quickly took my hand away and wiped away my tears.
"Yeah...yeah...I...", Man, I didn't know what to say. Seeing him again was literally a wish come true.
"You took some drugs or what?", Rohit asked, trying to control his laughter.
"I...I had a dream in which you went to fight in a war and died."

"Oh, come on! You know I even hate those war video games. You think I would go to war?...man you need to find yourself a girlfriend!"

Rohit burst into laughter soon after saying that. So did I. I felt so good because of it. It had been a long time since I smiled properly.

Then, I looked at my watch: 5:22.

It was time to get in.

"Yeah yeah, I won't be getting a girlfriend, let's go inside it's five twenty-two already."

"Whatever you say Mr.addict"

I really did miss him a lot. I missed laughing with him. I am so glad that I got this chance to be friends with him again. I was not going to let him go to war again, have his family die because of the bombings, or let the world war happen in the first place.

But how would I even prevent the war?

We headed inside the building. It was your typical small business complex.

A jeweller shop on the ground floor with lines of 'Xerox' shops to its right, a computer repair shop and a paan waala selling—you guessed it—paan.

The tuition, 'Praveen sir's classes for high school' was on the first floor of the building. The entire first floor had been bought by Praveen sir and his family. He started his tuition in 2013 and has so far made an army of teachers who are all excellent in their subjects. Praveen sir taught us physics and mathematics.

We entered the classroom and sat down on the second bench. I looked around the classroom. It was a small classroom with a single row of benches with some space to walk to the right. The benches were large enough for three people to sit comfortably. And there was a whiteboard in the front. The walls were beige, with four tube lights on all sides of the room.

So very nostalgic. Yet I was living this nostalgia.

I was sure I had finished the homework since I remember that I always did all the homework before going to sleep. But I was not sure if I had kept the right books, so I decided to ask Rohit about it.

"It's Praveen sir's class today, right?"

"Yeah, we're starting trigonometry today."

"Oh, right!"

Yeah, I remembered now how enthusiastic Praveen sir was today. I remember him telling us that this is his favourite chapter to teach in all of mathematics.

He had brought some ridiculously large protractors to teach us today, or rather, he will be bringing them.

Soon he entered the class with an enormous box in his hand, smiling widely.

"Hello Kids!", He shouted with his poised voice, which never failed to grab our attention.

"Good evening, sir!" we all said in unison.

"Alright take out your books."

He then fastidiously took out those protractors and began explaining.

It was a bit boring for me since I had already done all this...but it was very nostalgic. Seeing Praveen sir teach with so much passion was galvanizing enough to make anyone study with focus.

Nostalgic as it was, it also made me realize that I was going to be a topper now. I revelled in the fact that I was probably the smartest person here.

The class finished at 8:00 pm; we said our goodbyes and proceeded to go home.

The cars on the street with their shimmering bodies reflected the lights from the restaurants and street-food seller stalls.

The lights tempted me to look at the moon. Had the whole universe turned back in time?
I reached home by 8:15.
Mom had made palak paneer today.
"Hey, your eyes are watering! Is the dish too spicy today?"
"No No, just a little hot."
"Eat carefully Anirudh."

The dish was not too hot. It was just that it had been far too long since I had food made by my mother.

After getting a job I had to shift to Pune and I only occasionally went back to Mumbai for birthdays and certain festivals, and even then we simply ordered out.

After that, I went to bed. I was not sure if I would wake up in the same bed, or the same year. But if I did...I still would have no solid explanation as to why, or how I am here. Maybe God did this or maybe it was some kind of physics phenomenon that happens during a nuclear blast and we are not aware of it. But the fact was that I was in 2019, and I was probably going to stay here for a while...maybe. And that is all that mattered. Me being here was all I needed. I was happy.
But a concerning thought popped up: What happened to the actual Anirudh? The Anirudh of the past, whose body I have currently occupied. Had I replaced him? What exactly had happened?
I brushed the thought away and went to sleep.

This Is Real

III

Dreams are strange. They can be extremely vivid at times. So vivid that it feels like something that happened in a dream had happened in real life. Although you don't remember most of your dreams, some of them can just feel real and seem like a distant memory. But sometimes you want your dreams to be real. And it is these dreams that slowly make you lose your sense of reality, and you slowly start living in a fantasy world. But was I living in a fantasy world? A world cooked up by some writer, to satisfy his or her boredom?

The alarm on my digital clock went off. I received this clock as a gift on my seventh birthday from my grandmother. I always took that clock with me wherever I went (trips, junior college and when I shifted to Pune for work). I stopped the alarm. "6:00 am," the clock read.

I remembered everything that had happened. The attack, me supposedly travelling back in time, it felt real...it was too long...the pain from the blast and the shockwave...I could still feel it. It couldn't just be a dream or some fantasy.

I got up from my bed and went to turn the lights on. They were located near the door of my room. I reached the door, put my hand on the wall, and searched for the switch, But I couldn't find it. I frantically searched up and down the wall, but nothing. Then I remembered: I was no longer in Pune, but in my old house. I was just reminiscing about all the events that had happened, but my silly muscle memory thought it was still in Pune. It was no dreams

I stood there for a while.

I had slept through the night in my old house. I had eaten my mother's food; I had talked with my supposedly dead best friend. I did all of that. And all of it was real. It had to be.

I was back in 2019. There couldn't be any other explanation as to what was happening. And I hoped that there was no other explanation; I had somehow travelled back in time to 2019. No, my consciousness had travelled back in time to 2019. How did I travel back? I don't know, and I don't care. All I know is that I am here, and I will cherish every single second here. I am going to meet all my friends, spend more time with my family and I shall have no regrets. Maybe I will tell Rohit about this. It would be a lot of fun to make 'predictions' with him. I don't know when I should tell him, but I will tell him soon. Not that he would believe me.

The switch should have been near my desk. I turned around and went to my desk. My eyes had now adjusted to the dark, and I could easily locate the switch. I turned the lights on. My pupils took some time to adjust. But soon I could see that this still was my old room. The bed lying horizontally in front of me stuck to the wall. Above it, on the soft white walls, was a painting of a forest and a lake I had made with my mom. There was a window at the bottom of the bed, and a small table attached to a big wardrobe behind the small headrest of the bed. To my right, the wardrobe ended with the wall where I had searched for the switch, and then the door. Behind me was my wooden desk.

On it were a few old novels and a small table lamp. And, of course, a chair with the table. The desk was in the corner of the room, next to the window. It was a full-length window that covered the whole wall, leaving some space for the pillars.

I had to go to school now. The clock read "6:08 am". I quickly opened my wardrobe, took out my bag, and packed it. I checked my school calendar for anything I might have to do today. Oh yeah, the stand-up comedy competition was today! It wasn't my thing though, so I had decided not to participate in it.

I kept the calendar in my bag, took my clothes, and headed toward the bathroom. By the time I was out, my mother had woken up and was ironing my school uniform in my room.

"Good morning," she said softly, not wanting to wake up my father in the next room.

"Good morning," I whispered.

I changed into my uniform and sat to eat my breakfast, which consisted of cornflakes with milk and some chocos.

I went to school by bus, which came at around 7:30 in the morning.

I was now standing at my bus stop, which was at the corner of the street near my tuition classes. And soon there it was, the yellow metal box waddling around the potholes. It came to a halt in front of me.

Flashes of memories of the bus I tried to escape the blast came in front of me. But I brushed them off. I was no longer there. I was in 2019.

I sat in the second last seat, where all the 'big boys and gals' like me sat. I had a huge grin on my face while looking outside the window, like a child seeing some guy wearing a Mickey Mouse costume. The trees passed by. The cool morning breeze wrapped my head in a blanket of cold, and as my head rested on the bars of the window, my teeth clattered slightly with the vibrations of the bus engine racing through my skull.

Then, after winding around the neighbourhood, and picking up other students, the bus finally reached Rohit's stop.
"Yo wassup!"

Rohit shouted as he came down the aisle speed walking, with his hand in the air.

I gave him a high five, and he sat in the seat behind me. Then I turned around and said, "Nothing much, just going to school."
"Yeah, me too! Man, we have so much in common! We should be friends!" And we both laughed.
Then Rohit said, "Hey did you prepare for today's competition?"
"Nah, it's not my thing, really."
"Yeah, me neither. I had almost forgotten about it. Who do you think is gonna win? I think Harshil is going to win. He's always been pretty funny."
"I already know who's gonna win. It's Varun."

Gulp, I shouldn't have said that. Of course, I know who's going to win. I'm from the future!
"Huh? How do you know he's going to win?"
"I...uh...read his script."
"When?"
"Yesterday, he sent it to me to get my opinion."
"Your opinion?"
"Yeah, it is a bit weird…"
"Lol looks like you're cheating on your bestie," Rohit smiled mischievously.
"What, are you a four-year-old?" And we laughed some more at our lame jokes. That was close, though. I needed to be more careful. I was not ready to tell him yet.

We continued our conversation, talking about our class teacher, and making jokes about him and our mathematics teacher.

I was so engrossed with talking to Rohit that the ride to school felt like it lasted only a minute.

We reached school around 8:20. It was a decently reputed school, not very costly, but not very bad. Sure, the walls could be repainted, and the toilets and classroom walls could be cleaned for once, but I had mostly good memories from this school. Especially from my tenth standard. And a few regrets, but I thought I could work on those regrets now that I was back here.

The classroom was right next to the main staircase on the fourth floor. As you entered through the door, the window was right in front of you, the blackboard to your right, and rows of benches to the left. The peach-coloured walls had a lot of scribbles on them. All those ink stains made the walls look like artistic impressions, but they were really 'Raju loves Sanju' messages.

And on the third bench in the row closest to the window was my high school crush, Akriti.

My heart started pounding. I couldn't think of anything. I was just staring at her. She was reading a novel. Her hair swayed slightly from the breeze, making a few strands cover her eyes. She lifted her hand to brush them aside and then turned the page. The sun partly lit up her face, making it look like it had been made up of gold. And then I turned away.

Did I look too long? It probably wasn't more than 2 seconds that I stared, but I was a 21-year-old adult in a 15-year-old body. Should I have these feelings? She was just a kid to me now...but she was someone who came into my dreams very often. She was and is my first love. I didn't think that I was going to do something about my feelings, but should I? Isn't the whole point of me accepting the fact that I am here in the past, about me undoing my regrets? This was not something that I should be thinking about alone, so I thought that I should talk about this with

Rohit. But it would mean that I will be revealing the fact to him that I am from the future. But would he believe me? Is it even worth convincing him for something like this? But I should. I already thought about this in the morning.

Since I was going to be here for a while probably, It was going to be too tempting to tell him about it. And like I said earlier, it would be a lot of fun. But the question remained. How do I convince him?

And then it struck me; since I was from the future, I could predict events with considerable accuracy! Like today's competition! I did say that it would be fun to make predictions with him. It is also the best...no, the only way to convince him. Though I did tell him that I read Varun's script, I didn't. I could tell him to ask Varun whether I read his script or not. It wouldn't completely convince him, but it would be a start.

Rohit had taken his seat and was talking with a classmate in the seat behind him.

"Dude, today's competition is being sponsored by that famous comedy club, right?", Said Prathamesh to Rohit.

"Oh yeah, the winner is going to get a chance to perform at their club! Which would also be uploaded to their channel."

"Yeah, winning this competition is a big deal...yo, Anirudh! Sit down, will you?"

I didn't remember Prathamesh as much. I didn't talk to him a lot. All I remember is that he loved playing the guitar. Rohit knew him well, though.

"Who do you think is going to win, Anirudh?"

Now that was just ridiculous. Do I have something written on my face that says, "This guy knows who is going to win the competition"? Granted, it was only the second time someone had asked me this question, it was a little frustrating.

"Yeah, I…"

Before I could speak, Rohit interrupted me and said, "Oh, he is sure that Varun is going to win, as he read his…"
I cut him off, "Yeah, about that, Rohit. Could I speak to you for a minute?"

I got up and pulled Rohit from his seat.
"What happened, dude? What's wrong with telling Prathamesh about it?"
"I didn't read Varun's script."
"Ok then, what's the big deal? Just tell him that you lied to me for fun."
"It's a bit more complicated than that…"

Suddenly, our class teacher came in and we had to take our seats.
"I'll tell you in the break. Just don't tell Prathamesh about it yet."
"Fine...but...never mind, we'll talk about it."

And then we took our seats. Our class teacher was a little strict. Not too strict, it was just that he didn't like too much noise in the classroom, and he made that very clear on our first day.
"Alright class, take out your physics textbook. And before we begin, I would like to tell you that today's competition…"
"Is cancelled?" Varun shouted from the back of the class.

"No, it's not cancelled. It's going to be held starting from the lunch break In the school auditorium. A little too excited, are we, Varun?"

The whole class erupted in laughter while looking at Varun, who scratched the back of his head, smiling awkwardly.
"Anyway, be ready to move as soon as the break begins."
"Yes, sir!" the whole class shouted.

There were three classes before the break. They were still very nostalgic and had me giddy with the realisation that I was surely going to be the top in class as I had already studied everything. Now, of course, I didn't remember everything, but it wouldn't take more than a glance at my notes to bring everything back into my mind.

The most painful part was taking notes. My hand started paining after the 3 periods.

Each period lasted 45 minutes. So after 2 hours and 15 minutes, the bell rang, and it was time to head to the auditorium. It was on the top floor of the school building.

The auditorium was huge–Capable of seating at least 500 people–A big stage in the front defined it. It was divided into two sections of seats with a walkway. They made the girls and boys sit in different sections from each other. There were windows on all sides except the wall connected to the stage.

"Now, my dear Anirudh, tell me what was that in the first period?" We were now in the auditorium and were getting comfortable in our seats.

"Yeah, there is something I need to tell you."

"Ah, so lemme guess. The competition has been fixed by Varun's dad, and you know something about it."

Was Varun's dad rich? Rohit is very cunning, but wrong.

"Well, I wish it was something as simple as that…"

I slowly turned my head to look outside the window, which overlooked the Mumbai suburbs. No one in this world had any idea that someone had travelled back in time, but Rohit was about to be that one person. The world from this point would start to change.

Then the teachers closed the window and drew the curtains to make the auditorium dark, and that was a sign for the competition to begin.

"Will you just tell me?"

I contemplated whether telling him was a good idea, but I had to tell him someday, right? Besides, I had gone through this train of thought before. There was no turning back now.

"I am from the future; 2025. That's how I know Varun is going to win."

Rohit stared at me with an annoyed expression on his face.

"Fine then, keep your secrets."

"Yeah, of course, you don't believe me. Just look at me. Do I look like I am lying to you?"

"Yeah."

"Ok, Varun's dad is not Mukesh Ambani. He can't just fix such a big competition."

"Bro, are you on drugs?"

"Just why do you think this competition would have been fixed?"

Rohit fell into a contemplative state with his gaze downwards. He squeezed and twisted his lower lip and then put his hands on his hips.

He finally looked up and said, "No, I don't see how fixing the competition would benefit the school or the comedy club, and yeah, Varun's dad is definitely not rich enough. But come on seriously. You're from the future?" Rohit continued in a laughing tone, "Even if you are from the future, how do you expect me to just accept that?"

"Because I'm your best friend?"

Rohit gave me a blank stare.

"Alright, you know what Anirudh? Let's see who wins!"

Rohit then looked ahead at the stage. Of course, he wouldn't believe me so easily. It would just take some time, I guess.

Only 15 students from the whole school participated, and they had been asked to speak for not more than 5 minutes. So the school had expected the competition to not take more than 2 periods. Most of the stand-ups weren't very funny, except 3 of them, including Varun's. The judges themselves were famous comedians and also did stand-up comedy at the end of the participants' 'speeches'.

The club was doing this competition to promote the opening of several of their cafes across Mumbai, and our school wasn't the only one where such a competition had been held. But it finally came to an end, and it was time to announce the results. One of the judges came onto the stage and spoke.

"What a school, such amazing students! I mean, if we had as much talent as y'all when we were your age, we would have reached the moon by now!"

"Stop that bullcrap and announce the winner already!" I shouted in my head.

"It was difficult for us to decide, but we have made our decision."

I was now sweating. What If I was wrong? What if the future had changed because of something extremely small that I unknowingly did?

"And the winner of the junior comedy king is…"

I bit my lips in nervousness. There was a lot of tension in the air.

"Varun Thakur!"

The whole auditorium shouted and clapped as Varun climbed up the stage to be felicitated. I looked at Rohit as he clapped with a smile on his face. I was sure that this wouldn't be enough to convince him, but it would put a doubt in his head.

And I probably shouldn't choose events close to me for predicting, as they have a higher chance of being accidentally changed by me. Something like the general elections would be a better event.

Rohit suddenly stopped clapping; the smile disappeared from his face. He turned his head, looked at me and exclaimed, "Damn, you were right!"

"Now, do you believe me?"

And with a big smile on his face, he said, "No."

Indian Predicted League

IV

"As you all know tomorrow is Sunday, and we finished 'life processes' a week ago. So tomorrow I am keeping a 20-mark test."

The entire class shouted, "No!" Not together all at once but it was enough to show their disappointment.

"Come on, guys, it is not going to be that tough, besides I am saving you all from Praveen sir's extra lecture." Said our biology teacher.

It was 5:30 pm now. And I was sitting beside Rohit in our tuition classes.

Today's class was on the control and coordination system of the human body. It made me realise how much of my 10th-standard biology I had forgotten. Tomorrow's test might prove to be difficult...it doesn't matter though, just one reading would be enough to make me remember everything!

At the end of the class, everyone outside was looking at their phones to know the score of today's IPL match.

Rohit hit my back and said, "Hey, time traveller! Do you know who is going to win today's match? Mumbai Indians or Sunrisers Hyderabad?"

"First of all, don't be so loud! Second of all, how do you expect me to remember a match that happened 7 years ago? But I have a hunch that it was the Mumbai Indians."

Rohit gave me a blank stare again, but after a few seconds, he said, "Alright, look, it's not funny. It never was. Just admit that you lied to me, felt bad about it and are trying to convince me that you are from the future!"

"Look bro, I am not lying to you right now. I did lie about having read Varun's script but that's it. You don't believe me now, but you will soon. Besides, you know I don't like pranks. And why would I make such a ruckus like a simple lie? Haven't you noticed weird and sudden changes in me from yesterday?"

Rohit sighed, then proceeded to stare at me for a few seconds, and said, "Fine, I believe you. You are my best friend, and you are not the kind of person who would play a prank on me like this. You did behave weirdly yesterday. The day before yesterday we were laughing about failing the board exams, but yesterday and today just felt different. I had this uncanny feeling coming off of you as if you were not you, but if what you are saying is right...It makes a bit of sense...look if you are playing a prank on me, now is the time to stop. Because if after a few days, you tell me it was a prank, I'm gonna kill you."

"I am not playing a prank on you, But I understand how you feel. I don't expect you to believe me right away, but I know that in time you will."

Rohit smiled and said, "Well, then it would be fun to have a time traveller as a friend."

"Yeah, we're gonna have so much fun!"

Looking back now. Rohit and I had a lot of fun together during our 10th standard.

Countless study sessions, spending more time playing than studying, going on night rides in Mridul Bhaiya's scooty, It is still hard to believe that I am here. I just hope Rohit understands and accepts the fact that I am from the future…and doesn't go to war.

After that, I went home, opened my book and studied for tomorrow's test. It took me very little time as I had already done this before. Parts of it were always there in my brain and I just needed to read my notes once, or maybe I was just overconfident. After that, I went to have dinner and started watching the match with my dad.

My dad is one of the most chill human beings you will ever meet, except if it's about studies. He is a financial consultant at a stock exchange. But yeah, surprisingly chill about things.

"136 is not going to be a big deal for Sunrisers." He said, drinking his fizzy drink which looked suspiciously like vodka, but he couldn't be drinking it that easily though, and he preferred beer anyway.

"Maybe, but I don't think MI is going to let them win very easily."

The second innings were about to start.

My mom was scrolling on her phone, but then she paused, looked at me and said, "Anirudh, you have a test tomorrow morning at 8:30?"

"Yeah, I studied for it before dinner."

Then my father chimed in and said, "Should you go to sleep then?"

"Yeah, goodnight."

"Goodnight," they said in unison; I got up and went straight to my bed.

If there is one thing that scares me about my dad, it is when he asks rhetorical questions like that. The fear didn't go away even after having a job.

Anyway, I had to go to bed.

We rarely remember our dreams. But when we do, they are not normal dreams; nightmares or dreams about our loved ones are the ones we do remember, though not for very long.

And that night I had a dream. A very bizarre and frightening one.
Everything was burning around me.
There was a bus upturned to my right.

It was night, but the whole sky had an orange glow. In front of me was something huge and metallic.

It was something that looked like a mosquito but with very thin legs and a huge bloated body. It was as tall as the Eiffel Tower. Thin wires were protruding from the head that spread around, growing and touching the ground as if it were looking for something. What's more frightening is that there were almost an infinite number of them all around me in the distance.

Then I heard a voice that sounded as if it came from behind my head. It sounded like a Russian oktavist. The voice reverberated and echoed as if the oktavist was singing in a cathedral. I looked back, but there was nothing. I couldn't understand what the voice said, but I could feel that it was talking to me.

Suddenly, massive lights appeared in front of me.

The metal mosquito was shining brightly, and it looked as if those thin wires coming out of its head were pulling it towards me. The voice continued, it started speaking faster, and another voice joined in, and another and another, until all I could hear was a wall of deep heavy whispering.
The ground shook with the metallic monstrosity falling, falling on me. But before it could...I woke up.
It was morning now. The sun was starting to rise, the sky a soothing blue. It calmed me down. I never had a dream that was so terrifying and vivid as this.

But then again, never before had I travelled back in time, either.

"This was just a nightmare," I thought to myself. But I've had nightmares before, and something just felt off about this one. I brushed it off and got out of bed to start my day.

I felt excited for the test as I walked towards the tuition building at 8 in the morning. The test was supposed to start at 8:30, so I walked as slowly as possible, enjoying the Sunday morning sun. It took me 20 minutes to get there. That was how slowly I was walking.

"So Mumbai Indians won, as you said."

"That was more of a guess and not a prediction. Varun winning? That was a prediction."

"Dude, they only made 136 runs but still managed to beat Sunrisers by 40 runs?"

"Bro, I don't remember this match even a single bit...wait a minute, didn't Mumbai Indians win the IPL in 2019?"

"Will win? You're scaring me, bro. Please tell me you are playing a prank."

"Nope, not a prank."

Rohit just looked confused now. He shrugged and said, "So, are you feeling nervous?"

"This is the first time I am giving a test in, like, 3 years. My job didn't require any writing work either."

I took out my pencil box and my writing pad and laid them on the table. Earlier it was just me and Rohit, but now four students had entered the classroom.

"Didn't we give our 9th standard final exa...oh right, you are from the future, how exceedingly convenient."

"Keep your voice down!" I whispered to him.

"Wait, a second. You said you came from 2025. How is it that you had a job? Shouldn't you be at a university or something?"

Yeah, he was right about that, but I had to just get a job after the 12th standard. I was not alone, though. Many people had fallen into the same predicament.

"Well, a lot happens in the future...a lot of people had to just get a job after 12th standard to get financial stability because of the..."

I stopped. Should I be telling him about the war and the pandemic now?

"Because of what?"

"Students keep your bags outside," said the invigilating teacher.

The class was almost full now. I think I would wait a little before revealing to him about the future dystopia.

I felt very nervous all of a sudden as we went to keep our bags.

"Come on! You have already done these things!" I thought to myself. It doesn't matter a single bit as to how much I scored on this test, but I still felt weird. I felt like I had forgotten everything. I still mustered up the courage and kept my bag outside.

20 minutes into the test.

And my sheet was blank.

I had indeed forgotten everything.

"You know you're going to fail," my invigilating teacher said to me, staring down disdainfully at my blank test paper.

Following that comment, the whole class erupted in laughter. Staring at me, not pointing fingers, but just laughing loudly.

"Alright class, focus on your paper!" The invigilator shouted at the class.

I got an intense sense of Déjà vu and with it; I felt a sudden extreme pain in my head. It felt like my head was about to burst. It only lasted for a second.

A few students were now handing in their papers and leaving the exam room. Even Rohit got up and gave his sheet to the invigilator. But before he went out, he said to me, "Just write 'OM' on the paper and come out. I am waiting for you outside." I raised my hand to hit him.

"You finished your paper, right? Move out!" The invigilator scolded Rohit, and he scurried out before I could hit him.

I looked at the question paper...and suddenly I could remember everything! I still had half an hour left, and could finish the paper if I hurried!

I started writing furiously. And finished the paper in the nick of time.

"Why did you wait for me to humiliate you in front of the class to write the paper?" The invigilator asked me with her eyes wide as I handed over the paper.

I apologised and left the room.

Rohit was standing near the staircase.

"How long was the OM?" He teased me, with a wide grin on his face.

"Oh, shut up! I completed the paper!"

"Yeah, sure!"

A sudden chill crawled down my spine, an eerie sensation that made it seem like someone was watching me. Then, that headache returned with a vengeance. It was as if needles were piercing my brain, the same unbearable pain from just half an hour ago. It felt like an immense force, akin to a colossal octopus, clenching my brain relentlessly, threatening to make it explode.

I couldn't take the pain anymore and lost my consciousness.

A Dream, A Nurse and A Strange Diagnosis

V

I was at the same place I had dreamt about yesterday. It was the most chilling dream of my life and something I didn't want to experience again. But here I was, standing next to the upturned bus, which was now on fire.

There was fire all around me as well. This place was a vast open field that stretched up to the horizon. Random buildings seemed to have risen from the ground, half-broken and burning. A few burning trees and bushes could also be seen.

But I didn't feel hot, quite the opposite: I felt very cold. Fortunately, There were no giant metallic creatures like last time. I shuddered just thinking of them.

But why was I here? I had just fainted, right?

It gave me extreme discomfort.

Did I die and go to hell?

That thought gave me goosebumps. My heart started beating rapidly. My hands started shaking; from the cold or fear? I didn't know.

"Wake up!", I screamed repeatedly at myself. My voice seemed to echo in the surroundings. The sight of all this destruction, this desolate landscape, was sickening me.

This had to be a dream. Maybe I was in a coma? This was all very strange.

I kept shouting to wake myself up as if that was ever going to work.

After a few minutes of shouting, I heard a voice. A very deep voice. I started walking in the direction it seemed to be coming from. It seemed to be repeating something. It started getting louder as I was presumably getting closer to it. It sounded similar to the voice of my previous dream.

I had walked for hours now, or so I thought. The voice was the only thing keeping me from falling to the ground. The only goal and the only hope were the dark and deep voice. I wanted to get out of here. And I felt that if I could understand the voice, I could go back. Yet there was that fear of confronting that voice that gnawed at me.

The voice was now loud enough for me to understand a few words.

"You...how..."

I started running, and the voice started becoming clearer.

"You...be...how are..."

And clearer.

"You shouldn't be...how are you..."

And then I stopped running, as it said in a crystal clear voice, "You shouldn't be here. How are you here?"

Then my body felt as if it was weightless, as if having been dropped from a great height. And I woke up sitting on what seemed to be a bed, with my lungs gasping for air. I was sweating from head to toe. I tried to breathe normally and tried to calm myself down.

"It was just...a dream?", I said to myself, still confused and scared. I never wanted to go there again. That dreadful place. Why did I dream of it?

You shouldn't be here. How are you here?

The words of the deep voice echoed in my ears.

What did that mean? I shouldn't have been to the place I was in my dream? Or in 2019? Probably the latter.

Something felt very wrong about all of this. Why was I in 2019 in the first place? I should have been dead.

But where was I now?

I was wearing some blue coloured clothes, and one of my fingers had a clip on it. The clip had a wire attached to it, which went to a machine to my right. The machine had graphs on it. A number in the corner and a label above it read, "heart rate." The room I was in had white marble walls with a squeaky ceiling fan above me.

I had to be in a hospital, but for how long was I out?

The door in front of me opened, and a nurse entered the room. But I couldn't believe my eyes when I saw her face.

"Akriti?" I said in disbelief.

"Hey! So you're awake Anirudh!"

"You're a nurse? Wha...what's today's date?"

"Well, you've been in a coma for fourteen years." She said that as she tilted her and smiled.

14 years? Impossible!

Then a middle-aged man wearing a white lab coat entered the room with a writing pad in his hand and started scolding Akriti. "Akriti! Is this how you treat a patient who has been under syncope? Giving him a shock?"

"But I know him."

"So? Haven't you learnt anything while you were here? You are very lucky to be here! Don't take it for granted, and follow protocols!"
"Yes, sorry, doctor. I won't do this again." Akriti looked a little sad.

The doctor sighed. He scratched his forehead and then looked at me.
"I am sorry about that. It's been only 3 hours since you fainted. Today's date is still 7th April 2019."

My mind became relaxed.
"Alright, let's take a look at you. So, what is the last thing you remember?"
"I remember talking to my best friend Rohit after taking the exam. Then I had this extremely painful headache. And then I don't remember anything."

I carefully left out the dream part. Don't want him to think I'm crazy or something...wait, am I? Has this time travel caused actual damage to my brain?
"On a scale of one to ten, how would you rate the pain of the headache?"
"15."

The doctor raised his eyebrows, and Akriti gave a small chuckle, to which the doctor looked at Akriti disappointedly and then proceeded to write something on his pad. He then took out a small flashlight and stretched my eyelids. He briefly shined some light in my eyes, making me flinch.

He again wrote something on his pad, and then asked me,
"Do you still feel any pain?"
"No."
"Ok, do you remember where you were born?"
"Gorakhpur."

"What was the name of your grandmother?"
"Suhasini Nair."
"What did you do the last weekend?"
Wait, what did I do last weekend? I was punching some numbers into an Excel sheet. I can't say that!
"I just studied," I replied hesitantly.

The doctor stared at me and nodded, before writing something in his notepad.
"Ok. So you don't seem to have any memory loss. That is a very good sign. A specialist will be with you shortly."

Then he turned to Akriti and asked, "Do you know where his parents are?"
"Yes."
"Good, then go bring them here. And don't try anything like that ever again. I know you are here to learn, but don't forget that this is a full-fledged hospital."
"Yes, sorry doctor."

The doctor left the room and so did Akriti. But before she closed the door, she popped her head from the door, and with that heartwarming smile of hers, she said, "Sorry!"

I was still bewildered because Akriti was working as a nurse in this hospital. And that too at this age? But the doctor said she was here to learn.

Soon my parents came in with Akriti. My mom was in tears.
"Annu!" she screamed and then rushed to the bed and hugged me. She then planted several kisses on my face.
"I am fine mom, you're embarrassing me."
"I am your mother! How could you do this to me?" She screamed.
Akriti was trying very hard to control her laughter.

My dad looked a little tense. But refrained from saying anything.

Then the door opened, and another doctor came with the previous one. I assumed he was the specialist.

My mother got up from the bed and went to stand beside Dad.

"Hello Anirudh, I am Dr Shishir. So we have taken your MRI and done some further testing. We are waiting for the results from two of the tests, which should arrive by this evening. Dr Vishal already confirmed that you don't seem to have any memory loss. I would still like to look at the neural imaging, however. But you had also fainted for an extremely long time than usual, yet don't show the signs of anything like a seizure, which is usually the case if a patient has fainted for more than 5 to 10 minutes without having any head injury. And patients feel extremely disorientated and weak. They can't even talk properly, let alone talk like you can."

Dr Shishir then turned to face my parents.

"The problem is that we haven't been able to identify the cause of his fainting. And all the tests we have done so far have declared him completely healthy. Initially, we thought that he had a seizure caused because of extreme amounts of stress, which is usually the case for patients his age, and he was also taking a test before this, which may have caused this. It could be dehydration, or there could be a problem with his heart, but so far, the test results don't point towards any of it. It truly is peculiar. So we would like to keep him under observation for two days, today and tomorrow. We would also conduct a few more tests."

"Yes, doctor." My mother said.

The doctor then faced me and asked, "So have you been having headaches often?"

"No, but I did have it during the test. Before it, I wasn't able to answer any questions on the paper and 20 minutes had passed. But then the headache came momentarily, and then I could answer everything and remember everything. I did have to rush the paper since I had less time. But honestly, I have given worse papers in worse conditions and nothing like this has ever happened."

In fact, in the coming years, I took a lot of even more stressful exams, and this issue never popped up.

"Yes, I understand that there is one more that is not making a lot of sense. Although I think it is more of a faulty test result than the truth...your body seems to be a little older than it should be. And there are signs of tissue ageing and reforming in your body as if you somehow aged rapidly and then you started becoming younger also very rapidly."

Now that was very interesting. I think this time travel has affected my 15-year-old body in a certain way. But it also sounds extremely weird at the same time.

Then my dad said, "Then would you be doing the test again? And what does this mean?

"Yes, we would be doing the test again, but I don't think it is easy to conclude what is exactly happening. But rest assured, the boy appears to be completely healthy. Often these kinds of patients have some kind of tumour or other cancerous growth, but we haven't noticed anything like that either."

"But couldn't there be some hidden growth that you cannot detect?" My father asked.

"With symptoms this profound, a tumour would be easy to detect, as it would have grown considerably. But again, the boy seems to be completely healthy. Although his vitamin D levels are lower than recommended, it's common for city people to have a deficiency in vitamin D, but that has nothing to do with his case.

I don't think there is anything to worry about, but we are trying to determine what went wrong."
"Thank you, doctor." My father said with his hand, making a namaste gesture.
"You're welcome, sir. Ok then Anirudh, don't think about it too much and rest. I have other patients to attend to, so I will be leaving now. And Akriti?"
"Yes, doctor?"
"You haven't been assigned a patient today, right? Since you already seem to know him, I think it would be a good idea to assign him to you. And his case would also be a good opportunity for you to learn. And I'll also have nurse Anita to assist you, though he doesn't require much looking after."
"Yes doctor, that would be great."
And then the doctors left the room after saying namaste.

My mother came and hugged me.
"At least you seem to be fine."
"Yes, Mom, don't worry. I am completely fine."
"Alright, Anirudh, I do have some work to do and your mother has to cook lunch, so we'll be leaving for now. Don't you take any stress you hear me?"
"Yes, Dad I won't."
Then my mother said to Akriti, "So are you his friend?"
"Not yet. We are just classmates. But I would like to be his friend!... I have never made any friends since I shifted to Mumbai last year."

I remember the first time I saw Akriti. She came to our school in around September 2018 (9th standard). She had shifted from Gujarat. She left a very lasting impression on me when she gave her introductory speech in front of the class. Her charming voice and an endearing way of conducting herself moved something in me. Her quirky laughing habit just felt different, yet so alluring. I wouldn't say it was love at first sight, but my adolescent self had fallen for her that day.

"Well then, today would be a good opportunity for you!"

"Yes, Aunty!"

And then my father chimed in and asked her, "But why are you working here as a nurse when you are in Anirudh's class?"

"I want to be a doctor, and my grandfather is the director of this hospital. So he gave me a chance to learn from the doctors here before I go to a medical college."

"Oh, wow! Anirudh should learn something from you!"

Akriti and my parents laughed while I lightly smacked my forehead, shaking my head.

Mom then gave me one last kiss on the forehead and said she would be back soon with lunch. My parents left the room, leaving me alone with Akriti.

"So you don't have a single friend here? How is that possible? I don't believe you, Akriti."

Akriti smiled a little awkwardly, and then said, "Yeah, it's true. The girls in the class have a circle of their own, and I never seemed to break into it. My housing society doesn't have anyone close to my age, so yeah, I don't have any friends."

"Well then, I will be your friend!" I said in possibly the most cheerful way.

"Oh, I am glad!"

She replied again with that heartwarming smile of hers and put her hand forward to shake my hand.

I also put my hand forward, and we shook hands.

Why did I never even try to talk to her before? She seems very easy to talk to.

Before all this time travel shenanigan, I was very afraid to talk to her, and I never did for the whole of 10th standard! And here I am making her a friend so easily!

Sudden Genius

VI

"Also, where am I?" I asked.

Akriti seemed to be astonished at hearing that question, but the astonishment soon turned into laughter, as she covered her mouth with her hand.

"Oh, yeah, no one told you that! Well, you are at the Chamunda hospital."

"So not very far from home. That's cool. This is a good hospital."

"Yeah, my grandfather put in every effort to make this place great. So you live nearby?"

"Yeah, Glory Heights Society. Where do you live?"

"Dude no way! I live in Marigold!"

"What? That's literally next to my building!"

"Small world, huh?"

How is that possible? So all this time, I have been living right next to her! How did I never come to know about this?

Did I travel into a parallel universe or something?

"But how do you come to school? I have never seen you on the bus."

"My father manages his clinic, which is near our school. So he drops me off while going to the clinic every morning."

"Wow. You're rich, huh?"

Akriti giggled.

"Yeah, you could say that, but only sort of. My father opened up his clinic along with his friend last year. My grandfather wanted to help him with the money, but my father refused. He wanted to be 'his own man'. So although my dad does make a lot of money, it goes into paying for the loans. But my grandfather is very rich. Before this, my dad used to work as a doctor in a hospital in Agra, but he always wanted to start a business. So we moved to Mumbai when he finally got the chance to start one. Grandpa had been calling us here for a long time, anyway. Also, everyone in my family is some kind of doctor. So yeah, you could say I am rich."

"That is so cool! So this is why you want to be a doctor! Since the rest of your family is one, they must have inspired you a lot!"

Akriti's face showed a touch of sadness. She was still smiling, but that cheeky, mischievous Akriti suddenly seemed downcast. She looked at the heart rate monitor and then told me something I wasn't prepared to hear.

"When I was seven, my mother had taken me to a fair. She drove our car to it. On the way back, something hit our car and my mother lost control of the car. I survived saved by my mother who herself...if only I were a doctor or had even a little medical knowledge, I could have saved her. Sure, I was but a little girl: there was not much I could have done. But that is the real reason I want to be a doctor. I don't care about what my relatives have achieved with their practice. I want to be someone who can save anyone in any kind of medical emergency."

She was only seven! I can't imagine what she went through! Her eyes seemed to hide an abyss of pain. No one deserves to go through this. I know what it feels like to lose a loved one. Moreover, to a certain extent, she even blames herself! Why would she tell me something so heavy at the first meet though? I guess she was a little too desperate to make friends.

"But, hey! I have my father, my grandfather, everyone in this hospital, and now I have you too!" she said, with that heartwarming

smile of hers back on her face. I felt so good the moment she said that. It was like a sense of relief.
"And that was the fastest I've ever made friends!"
She simpered and said, "Oh, me too!"

Suddenly, her phone buzzed. She picked it up: It was from Dr Shishir. They were ready to do more tests on me.

We got up and headed to a room that had large equipment. They did an MRI again, an EEG and a bunch of other tests. By the time they were done with the tests, it was lunchtime, and my mother was already here with lunch. Akriti said she had to go eat with her grandfather, so she gave me her phone number in case I needed anything, and left me with my mom, who then took me to my room.

My mother tried to feed me herself, but I refused and ate it by myself. I had already given her too much to worry about. I could at least eat by myself.

She stayed with me for the rest of the afternoon and tried to persuade me to go to sleep, but I didn't want to go to sleep. I didn't want to go to that place again. She said she had to go home as the maid was about to come and clean the house.
"Don't worry mom! I will be fine. You go."
"I won't until you are asleep."
"Fine, I'll sleep."

So I closed my eyes and pretended to sleep for 10 minutes. And it worked! Mom left thinking I was asleep...but then I fell asleep for real.
The sleep, however, was dreamless. No weird hellscape. Thank god.
I woke up to find Rohit sitting on a chair beside my bed, playing a game on his phone. The bed made some noise as I got up, alerting Rohit. He then closed the game and put his phone in his pocket.

"Hey, good morn...evening! So glad to see that you are fine."
"Yeah, you probably called the doctor, right? When I fainted."
"It was Praveen sir. I was too scared to do anything."

I guess it would have been quite scary to see a friend just faint like that. And especially if that friend is your best friend.

"But thank God, he was there. He practically rushed you to the hospital on his bike. No ambulances were called. It would have taken longer for the ambulance to come, so he just decided to take you as fast as he could."

"On a bike? Wow, I must thank him."

"Oh, definitely."

"What time is it?"

"Six-thirty pm, year twenty-twenty-five," Rohit said with a chuckle.

"Oh come on dude, you wouldn't be alive if it was twenty-twenty-five."

Gulp...shouldn't have said that.

"What? I will die?"

Rohit looked horrified. His eyes were wide. I quickly tried to change the topic.

"A lot happens in the future. But wait, you didn't tell anyone about me being a time traveller right? people will think I am crazy."

"No, I didn't tell anyone. No one believes you are crazy. I do have my doubts, but no, I didn't tell anyone. But you're saying I will die in the future. Before 2025? "

"You won't die. At least now, if I tell you how you'll die, you won't. And I am not crazy...probably, but look! Didn't I predict Varun winning the competition? And the Mumbai Indians winning the match?"

"You did do that. But they could simply be very good guesses for all I know. I do believe you, I want to, but you must realise that we can't rule out the possibility that there could be something wrong with you. But how do I die?"

He was quite persistent about knowing about his death. Anyone would be.

"I will tell you. Not now, but I will. Just relax for now and there is nothing wrong with me. Even the doctors can't figure out what's wrong with me. I seem to be completely healthy!"

"Yeah, I know. I talked with your dad. But I suggest you make bolder predictions now. Things that one simply can't guess. I do want to believe you. But there's not enough for me to believe you completely right now. I might have to tell the doctors about it eventually if I end up not believing you. You could be a psychopath who is plotting my death for all I know. Just tell me how I die. Why won't you?"

"You die while fighting in a war, happy?"

"Huh? War?"

"I will tell you a story about the future that will help you understand. But not here, and not now."

"Fine...at least make some predictions about events in April, so that you can make me believe in you."

"Let me think then."

I sat on the bed with my hands grazing my hair slowly. The soft hair seemed to be filled with electricity. I felt like I was getting static electric shocks. I tried to remember what had happened in my future past. Surprisingly, I could very sharply remember things! As if my brain wasn't my brain, but an internet search engine. I wandered around the galaxy of memories and every event that I had only briefly glanced at an article about, appeared as clear as a crystal in front of my eyes. I could have used this when the doctor was asking me questions!

"Today is 7th April right?" I asked.

"Yeah."
I searched for events that were about to happen recently.
"On 10th April, we will receive the first-ever photograph of a black hole. On 15th April, The Notre Dame Cathedral in Paris will catch fire. On 3rd May a cyclone called 'Fani' will make landfall in Odisha, and it will be the worst storm in Odisha since 1999. I could tell you more, but for now, I think this is enough. Oh, and do you need spoilers for endgame?"
Rohit was now staring at me with his face showing an expression of utter disbelief.
Then the door to the room opened, and Akriti entered the room. She also looked surprised.
Gulp...she probably heard everything.
"How much did you hear?"
"Everything! Dude, these walls are paper-thin! You need to be quiet about these things! People will think you are crazy!"
And then Rohit chimed in and said, "And you don't think he is crazy?"
"I did at first, but his test results have come in, and they would make complete sense if he was a time traveller. I have never seen Dr Shishir so baffled over a patient before. And the things Anirudh said only a moment ago..."
Rohit interrupted her and said, "And wait, Akriti? What are you doing here? In a nurse uniform?"
"She work-studies here. Her grandfather is the director of this hospital."
"Ok...I'll ask more about it later, but first, Anirudh? Those are *some* predictions! If they come true...Well, at least they are things that can't be just very good guesses. And uh...I guess Akriti knows about it too. And believes you?"

"I don't believe him. At least not yet, but if his predictions come true...I don't know then...but the test results would make sense if you are a time traveller...Oh, and the doctor would be here soon, we should stop talking about this. Maybe I should tell the doctor."
"Please, don't! At least not yet. Give me some time to prove myself. At least wait for those predictions!"

Akriti stared at me for a few seconds. She then gave a nod, giving rise to an awkward silence. I wanted to break the silence, but the doctor arrived. He had a sheet, a writing pad, and a pen in his hands.
"Anirudh! How are you feeling?"
"I feel alright. My test results came in and they're strange?"
"Very! They make no sense! But first."

He then handed me the pad and the pen and flipped the sheet so that the part containing the printed text was facing the surface of the pad, and the blank side was facing me. And now that I had the sheet with me, I realised that it had two sheets stapled together and not just a single sheet.
"Don't flip it yet. Only do it when I tell you. This contains fifty mathematical calculation questions. You will have 30 seconds to solve all of them."
50 questions? In 30 seconds? What? Does he want to give me a headache again?
Rohit looked horrified. Akriti just stared at the paper on the pad.
"But why? What is going on?"
"Don't worry, just think of it like any other test. Ready?"
I held the pen in my hand. I glanced at Rohit, who gave me a thumbs up with a concerned look on his face.
"Yes."
"OK, then."

Dr Shishir took out his phone, probably to turn on the timer.
"I will count backwards from three, and when I say 'go', you flip the papers and start solving. Understood?"
"Yes, doctor."
"OK then. 3, 2, 1...go!"

I flipped the page and started solving the paper. It was nothing too theoretically complex, just basic multiplication, division, addition and subtraction. But with ridiculously large numbers. Strangely though, my solving speed seemed to have increased a hundred times. I had never calculated anything so fast. This utter speed...I felt like my hand was flying. My brain felt like it was running on rocket fuel.

185189×96=17778144

151÷3464=0.043591224

One by one I looked at each question, and the answers just appeared as fast as a photon. It wasn't like someone was displaying the answers in my eyes. I did feel like I was solving it, but...
"And stop!", Dr Shishir yelled. I immediately dropped the pen and took some deep breaths.

I could complete 41 out of the 50 questions...wow! This was unbelievable!

Dr Shishir took the paper. And looked at another paper that he took out of his pocket. His gaze went back and forth between the two papers. After some time, he put the paper down and looked at me.
"Anirudh, you solved forty-one questions out of 50...but your answers are all correct! I can't believe this!"

Akriti took the paper and looked at it. Rohit Also got up to look at it. And then they simultaneously turned their heads and looked at me, dumbfounded.

"I am surprised too," I said.

The doctor asked, "This is not making sense. Have you ever done something like this before?"

"No." but then the memories of this morning's test flashed before me.

"Actually...When I was taking the test in the morning, a similar thing happened after the headache."

"Yes, you did talk about that. Look, your brain is showing tremendous amounts of activity. Also, there is another thing that does not make sense. Your body seems to be older than it should be. I told you this before, but it's confirmed now."

Akriti momentarily raised her eyebrows at me, as if trying to say, "Yeah, this is what I was talking about."

"So, what does this mean?"

"I don't know...I am going to send your case to my colleagues. Also, I don't think there is a need to keep you under observation, you will be discharged at nine pm today."

"Oh, that is great! So there is nothing to worry about?"

"As of now, no. However, I would suggest you contact a nutritionist to take care of your slight vitamin D deficiency. But I would request you to come for a full body checkup again after three months, and keep coming every three months."

"Ok, doctor."

And then the doctor left in a hurry. His answers to my questions were also erratic, as he immediately changed the subject.

If he was discharging me, then everything should be correct. But shouldn't he keep me now to learn more now that he has confirmed that I am suddenly a genius? And my body is older than it should be?

Rohit was staring at the ceiling while twisting his lips. He then looked down and asked, "So, you're a genius now? how?"

"I don't know," I replied. Akriti said, "Your body is older than it should be. I mean, it could mean anything...but...I don't know anymore. Also, is there some kind of device in the future that makes you smarter? And where are you from? How did you get here?"

It looked like she was almost convinced too now. Although, only on the surface. Something seemed odd about her behaviour, but I nudged my thoughts away. It was probably just me overthinking.

"Yeah, Anirudh, how did you time travel? Where's the time machine?" Rohit asked.

"First of all, I am from 2025. there is no technological development in 2025 that could make you instantly smarter. Secondly, I didn't travel, I think only my mind travelled. But my body is older? So I guess parts of my body also travelled? I don't know. And thirdly, I didn't use a time machine or any kind of machine...I guess I did technically use a bus...The last thing I remember is a nuclear explosion, and then I was here."

Rohit asked, "So you don't have any clue as to how you got here? Or why you are a genius suddenly?"

"No."

Akriti blurted out, "Wait, nuclear explosion? And earlier you said that Rohit wouldn't be alive if it were 2025. Just what happens in the future?"

Both their faces were glaring at me in anticipation.

"Fine, I will tell you about the future. I was not going to say this yet, but you won't stop asking me questions. Also, you might wanna sit down."

They both took a seat. Their posture showed uneasiness. You could feel the fear and confusion in the room. A lot was about to be revealed.

I also realised the gravity of what was going to happen. I was going to reveal the truth to the world now. This meant that I was going to change the future. I was going to prevent Rohit's death simply by telling him about what was going to happen in the future.

A Story of the Future

VII

"I am going to try to keep it short, so here we go," I said, adjusting my posture to sit straight. Rohit and Akriti were watching me like a hawk.

"It all began in Wuhan, China. A 'viral pneumonia' is discovered in November this year that later becomes a pandemic."

"A pandemic!" Rohit screams.

"Dude! Don't shout! Keep your voices low, both of you."

"Sorry," Rohit said softly.

"Anyway, go ahead," Akriti said in a whispery voice.

Moreover, I changed my tone to a lower voice while stating, "The virus responsible for this will be named SARS-CoV-2, and it shares similarities with the SARS-COV-1 virus that emerged from 2002 to 2004. I started speaking in a lower voice as well, "The virus causing it will be called SARS-CoV-2 which is related to the SARS-COV-1 virus that happened from 2002 to 2004. They belong to the same family of coronaviruses. The disease will be named COVID-19, and it is an upper respiratory disease. The first wave that starts spreading around the world in March 2022, is not that bad. The disease causes a lot of deaths (the mortality being 3%)

but a lot of people recover as well. The scary thing about it is its infection rate. It is more infectious than a common cold. *Too infectious.* The US suspected that COVID-19 was a laboratory leak, similar to the SARS outbreak. China denied it and we could never prove it. The worst thing, though, will be the economic breakdown. Hundreds of thousands of people will lose their jobs as companies lay off employees to compensate for the lost profit as governments all around the globe impose lockdowns. Many small businesses will have to shut down as well."

"That doesn't sound good..." Rohit said.

"It's the least horrifying thing, though. In 2021, US troops withdraw from Afghanistan, but then the terrorist organisation 'Taliban' took over the country completely through force. This happened after Joe Bidden becomes the President after Trump looses the elections. Then there is the whole Israel-Palestine conflict, an Iranian major general is killed by the USA, adding to Iran's hate of the West. And a lot of bad things happen in the US as well, but it does not have any direct effect on the war, so I am gonna skip that part."

"The war?" Akriti asks.

"Yes, World War 3."

I expected them to show an expression of fear, but I noticed exactly the opposite. Rohit was smiling now.

"Really, Anirudh? World War 3? Then what will happen? An alien invasion?"

Akriti also laughed, covering her face with her hand.

"Yeah, you continue, Anirudh," she said with a pseudo-serious expression.

"Before the war, there will be a skirmish between India and China in 2021 in the disputed Galwan valley. This would become the inevitable catalyst for India to put the 'quad'-an alliance between the USA, India, Australia and Japan into action, as they conduct various summits and military practice exercises. This angers China, but they do nothing for now. In September 2021, The president of Ukraine approved a new national security strategy which includes a partnership with NATO. Russia doesn't like it at all. And in Feb of 2022, right after the Beijing Winter Olympics, Russia invades Ukraine."

"So that begins the world war?" Akriti asks.

"No, it merely acts as a catalyst."

"And what about the pandemic?" Rohit asks.

"The second wave of the pandemic comes In May 2021 and is very deadly. Oxygen cylinders and hospital beds become scarce as the medical system is overwhelmed. Vaccines are developed though and a huge amount of people get vaccinated and the pandemic gets very weak because of a mild strain of the virus by 2022. China, however, faces a huge problem. China had gone COVID-free for a very long time but as it opens its gates back, the infections start increasing. And Xi Jin Ping wants to push his 'zero COVID policy'. So he imposes severe lockdowns in Shanghai and other parts of China, which makes it a living hell. There is widespread civil unrest."

"Woah," Rohit said.

"Meanwhile, a lot of people have died in Ukraine. Other countries do not offer military force to help Ukraine, as they fear starting World War 3. They only offer weapons and accept refugees from Ukraine. The USA imposes severe economic sanctions on Russia. Countries all around the world, but mainly European countries, seize all properties and yachts of Russian oligarchs. India, however, is an excellent ally of Russia, so it abstains from voting against Russia in the United Nations. The USA keeps pressuring us. But we don't give in. In the end, they realise why we are abstaining: China. Russia gives us weapons at a fairly lower cost than the USA. These weapons are crucial in defending against China. Following the Ukraine war, there is a huge economic recession around the World. People were already struggling because of the pandemic, and now it gets worse. Even my dad loses his job."

"So that is why you had to get a job after 12th," Rohit said. Akriti looked confused, so Rohit continued, "Yeah, Anirudh told me about it this morning, but before I could ask him further, we had to give the test."

Akriti nodded her head.

"Yeah, I didn't get a job immediately after 12th as my dad tried to look for other jobs...in 2023 World War 3 started and job opportunities were severely reduced. I had no choice but to get a job to support my family and drop out of college. My dad got a job in an accounting firm, but they couldn't pay him a lot. This happened to a lot of people, but not your family, Rohit. Your family becomes wealthy. And your family helps us a lot. The main reason my father and I could get a job was because of your dad."

"I don't know what to say..." Rohit said. Surely it was a tough time for my family. Rohit was a gem of a friend to have.

"That's horrible..." Akriti said, "But how does the world war start then?"

"By the end of 2022, Russia gets half of Ukraine. There is an agreement and the Ukraine war stops momentarily. But Xi Jin Ping dies mysteriously, and Chen Miner takes over for him. Things deteriorate from there and the world war begins. It doesn't look like a world war, as the incidents to follow are isolated. But chaos ends up taking over the world and we start destroying each other for no reason except to gain stability, which actually causes more instability. The people of Russia are revolting, so in an attempt to gain back stability, Russia breaks the agreement and invades western Ukraine with full force, saying that Ukraine broke the agreement first and ended up capturing about 3/4th of the country by

March 2023. While the West is busy with Ukraine, China invades Taiwan. The U.S.A. again doesn't send its military but imposes sanctions on China. This time India votes against China. Russia, however, is completely cut off from the world. Every social media has stopped its services In Russia. Hence, nothing goes in or out of the country. Even VPNs stop working. Meanwhile, Sri Lanka and Pakistan have gone completely bankrupt. They look to India for help. India helps Sri Lanka but is reluctant to help Pakistan because debates in the parliament delay everything. By May 2023, Ukraine was completely annexed. And Taiwan has also been captured. A civil war erupts in Russia. China takes advantage of this and tries to capture eastern Russia, but fails as India helps Russia. So China starts strife in Kashmir and sends its navy in stealth to the Bay of Bengal. However, Japan identifies the fleet and intercepts it. There is a misunderstanding that the ships were coming to the Spratly Islands, which harbour a lot of resources in the Pacific Ocean. Japan loses one of its destroyers, and Japan and China enter a full-fledged war. Meanwhile, Russia tries to capture Poland in an attempt to unite its people. And the NATO alliance has no choice but to send troops there. China promises to forget all of Sri Lanka's and Pakistan's debt if they help China against India. And although it's unclear, China pushes North Korea to invade South Korea, and it does! China withdraws from Kashmir, to focus on the battle in the Pacific Ocean with Japan. Only for Pakistan to begin its fight with India, because this would mean they would no longer have to pay the debt to China. Sri Lanka goes into a civil war. Pakistan and India both bomb each other, but India ended up winning over Pakistan and taking over the country. Surprisingly, Russia and China join hands and they almost end up defeating Japan however, the quad is in motion and Australia and the USA finally send their navy into Japan along with India. Iran, Iraq, the

Taliban and most of the Middle East, except Israel side with China. Yemen with the Houthi rebels is a complete mess. The rebels try several times to stop the trade ships from going through the Red Sea, but the troops of the US, France and China stationed in Djibouti stop that from happening. In Israel, the internal Israel-Palestine conflict has become more profound, and the US has to focus more on that. Saudi Arabia sides with America, but the government is overthrown by ISIS in conjunction with Iran. World War 3 has officially begun. The UN tries to initiate peace talks all around, but it can't stop the war. The only thing it does is try to resolve the conflict in Israel and make countries come under a mutual agreement to not use nuclear weapons. But it is just a foot in the mud as you can't really believe that they won't"

Akriti and Rohit appeared dumbfounded.

"Woah!" Rohit exclaimed.

"And what about Africa? And Latin America?" Akriti asked.

"Much of Africa doesn't participate in war, most of Africa being pro-China. The food crisis is worsening in Africa. Famines have become a daily occurrence. Madagascar doesn't let India set up a base there, which might be a problem if China enters the Indian Ocean. South Africa becomes the UN's secondary headquarters and is very helpful in dealing with the famines in Africa. Africa also helps ensure that sea shipment routes are working despite the war...which proves to be a very hard job as some ports are owned by China and a lot of mines are also owned by China. Latin America doesn't do much besides allowing The USA to set up military bases. However, Mexico has become a hub for Russian and Chinese hackers and spies. The USA has to end up closing its borders completely to Mexico. Cuba and Brazil disagree with letting any country set up anything in their country. These parts of the world do remain somewhat neutral, but the economic effects of the war are amplified here. The UN can't stop the war, so it primarily focuses on providing humanitarian aid, operating mainly from Africa and Brazil."

"OK...sounds made up honestly...but OK," Akriti said. yes, of course, it sounds made up.

"So how do I die?" Rohit asked.

I took a deep breath and continued.

"It's 2024, and you are studying in Berkeley. The Middle East decides to bomb the whole of Europe along with sending its troops there. There is fighting everywhere. Even Switzerland, which has been neutral for a long time has to participate along with Germany, France, Finland, Norway, Spain and Portugal. Rohit's family dies in the bombings."

I looked at Rohit. Anger and sadness filled my eyes. Memories of holding Rohit's body at the port filled my mind, And I raised my voice a little.

"You come back to India, and despite my repeated protests you join the army and then go and die in the war."

I tried to calm myself down. It's not going to happen again. I will stop him from going to Berkeley.

Rohit was staring at me. After half a minute of staring, he said, "I guess that explains your behaviour on 5th April."

"Yeah, you get it? Don't you dare go to war!"

Then Akriti said, "We will all make sure the war doesn't take place in the first place."

"And how will we do that?" Rohit asked.

"I don't know right now, but we must figure something out, right Anirudh? And besides, we don't even know if you really are a time traveller… anyway, continue."

"Right. So...things escalate. Society, as we know it, has fallen completely, and no one is safe anywhere. The economy has collapsed, and food has been rationed for everyone. there are numerous cyber attacks everywhere, from banks to your local police station. Propaganda posts litter every social media. The West keeps pushing that the SARS-CoV-2 was a biological weapon, However in reality no biological weapons were used in this war. The biological weapons did exist, but there was no way of controlling them for now at least. People were very afraid regarding the usage of biological weapons in the future. But even more terrifying was the fear of a nuclear attack. Although no one thought it would happen...in 2025, it did happen. Now I don't know how the nuclear attacks happened. There was too much confusion on the night it happened. And very few news sources were operating at that time. I only realised that it had happened when my roommate woke me up saying that we needed to evacuate, and I saw a huge mushroom cloud in the distance through my window. DRDO had developed an advanced warning system which was installed in all phones. It was AI-controlled and gave us warnings and notifications about the war. It collected data from various sources, like satellites, government resources, social media and whatnot, to warn users of incoming missiles and other possible dangers. That night it warned us about the attack and gave everyone a notification to evacuate. However, it was too late. The news sources first said that only Mumbai had been nuked, but later when I checked my phone on a bus while evacuating it said, that at least 3000 nukes had been detonated all around the world. They said that the first strike was issued by China, based on a false alarm, But things were extremely unclear. Before I could gather more information, a nuclear attack happened in Pune, where I was...and I should have died there...but here I am."

"So you don't know anything about the world-ending scenario," Rohit said.

"No."

"Or how you travelled back in time? Or how your brain is working so fast?"

"No."

There was silence in the room for quite some time. Rohit and Akriti seemed to be processing what I had just told them. It surely was a lot to take in.

Akriti cleared her throat and said, "To sum it up. The pandemic will create an economic and social environment that will lead to a chaotic world and this chaotic world would have isolated incidents, which in the bigger picture will cause World War 3."

"Exactly," I said.

"Well, then we must prevent it," Rohit said.

Akriti waved her hand at us and said, "But first, we need Anirudh's predictions for April to come true."

"Yeah, I believe you Anirudh after all you're my best friend. Your story sounds far-fetched, but if your predictions turn out to be true, we must warn the world. And honestly, you're not lying. You seem to be believing the story that you told us. You could be delusional, but that will get cleared up through the April predictions. We must prevent the war."

"Right," Akriti said. She looked at Rohit in a begrudgingly. I don't think they believed me at all.

"Yes, we absolutely will," I told Rohit, looking straight into his eyes. Even if they didn't believe me, I needed to be firm in my beliefs. Wait, 'beliefs'? What was I thinking? These events did happen!

"Well, enough of the doom talk...Akriti, you are a nurse here?" Rohit asked.

Akriti laughed and started explaining to Rohit. Everything appeared to be in slow motion for me. Akriti's and Rohit's lips moved slowly. The room seemed to have a golden glow. This friendship seemed to be a fragile one. And I was afraid that I would end up losing these two wonderful people. The world looked scary. And it was about to become more frightening. But should I move forward? Maybe I should just enjoy this friendship and not do anything about the coming war and pandemic. Maybe I should just enjoy this while it lasts. The images of Rohit's dead body flooded my brain again. I was scared.
Uneasiness filled my chest.

A Revelation A Realisation

VIII

The next day at school, I was looking at the contents of my tiffin box. Mom had made soft rotis along with potato-chickpea curry. The brownish-red gravy tasted spicy, yet sweet. The airtight box released puffs of steam when opened, releasing the invigorating aroma of the dish. The soft potato and crunchy chickpea gravy filled my mouth with joy. The rotis were also another level of heaven. They felt like touching a pillow and when you tore the roti; it felt like cutting a piece of linen cloth with scissors. It's amusing how it's the little things like these that I yearned for when I began my job.

"Two days," Akriti said.

"Two days," I repeated, nodding my head.

Two days from today, NASA was going to release the first-ever picture of a black hole.

Then Rohit said, "Wait, listen, I searched about the first black hole picture. I found a few articles that say that we could be receiving the first picture of a black hole on Wednesday. If we do, then this would again be just a very good guess. You might have seen an article and made this prediction."

"Yeah, but what those articles won't tell you is that there would be a press conference about it."

"Of course, there would be a press conference, Anirudh!" Akriti shouted. The whole class was staring at us. But after looking at our embarrassed faces, they continued with their verbal musings. Akriti widened her mouth in a grimace. "Gotta be careful," she said, tilting her head.

"It does look like I am lying. I am not." I said.

"Look Anirudh," Rohit said, "we are just scared for you. You could be delusional. There could be something mentally wrong with you. But I do agree that there are things that can't be explained *at the moment.* However, it is more likely that you are mentally ill than you are a time traveller."

"All I ask of you two is to have patience. Remember what I said about 15th April? Notre Dame burning?"

Then Akriti said, "Yeah, that seems like a promising prediction. Only if you're not bluffing about everything. On the 15th you will be like," Then Akriti contorted her face in a funny-looking way and continued, "haha, Akriti and Rohit, you two are such fools for believing that I am a time traveller, haha. Or something like that."

Rohit and I laughed at Akriti's humorous impression of me.

"No, I won't say that! And what's up with that ridiculous impression?" I said, trying to control my laughter, but Rohit burst into laughter as soon as I said that. He laughed for a good 20 seconds.

"Oh, come on, it wasn't that funny," Akriti protested.

"Yeah, sorry. It's just your face..." Then Rohit burst into laughter yet again. I couldn't help but laugh, too. And so did Akriti, covering her face in embarrassment

"Anyway," Rohit said, "why don't you use that genius brain of yours and think of something that happens today? It doesn't have to be something big. Even something like Akriti tripping and falling on her head would do. "

"Hey!" Akriti punched Rohit on the shoulder. Rohit started giggling.
"Oh, yeah, Akriti falls off her bench and then her books fall on her."
"Oh, come on Anirudh!" Akriti growled.
"The point is that 15th April is still, what?" Rohit said.
"7 days away, on Sunday," I said.
"Right. You expect us to wait for a week to sell you off to the psychiatric hospital?"
Now Akriti started laughing. She said, "Drop books on me now, Anirudh! ha!" Rohit gave a small chuckle and smiled.
"Fine, I'll think of something that happens today."
"Yeah, now you don't laugh at my joke and just smile!" Akriti said to Rohit
"Eh, you call that a joke? And first of all, I made the joke about the psychiatric hospital."

Rohit and Akriti continued their bickering while I fell into a contemplative state.

Although I had decided against predictions about events close to me, these two had as much patience as fans at a Travis Scott concert...So I had to think of something.

I again dived deep into my memory galaxy. I searched for the memories of 8th April 2019. And I got a few incidents. I was the one grinning now.
"What are you grinning for?" Rohit asked.
"Today is Vandana ma'am's class, right? After the break?" I asked.
"Yes, Very nice prediction Anirudh," Akriti smugly replied.
"Today she is going to start the chapter 'Molder's Mirage' and she is going to ask Manas to read."
"Oh, that extract from the fantasy novel by the same name?" Akriti said.

"Yeah, there are some South Indian names and Manas is going to butcher them. It will be hilarious."
"On Purpose?" Rohit asked.
"No. And after that, she will ask Prathamesh to read, but he wouldn't have been paying attention." I said, the grin on my face as wide as an aeroplane. "But tell me, how would I have guessed that?"

Rohit and Akriti fell silent. They were supposedly thinking of a way to explain how I would know that. Rohit twisted his lips again. Why does he do that every time he's thinking?
"I don't know Anriudh, do you have anything else?" Rohit Asked.
"Yes! Today in the sports period, we boys will be playing Kabaddi. and the girls will be playing tennis. The funny thing is the period would end before we have even started the matches. We took too much time to make teams. Abhinaya will win two matches straight in a row among the girls."
Both Akriti and Rohit were staring at me with their eyes wide.
"Dude, how do you remember this?" Akriti asked.
"I don't know. Ever since the headache during the exam yesterday, my brain and body sort of feel different?"

Since I woke up this morning, my body has felt significantly different. With each breath, I could feel the wind going down my windpipe into my lungs and my lungs contracting and expanding with diaphragm muscles. I could feel the blood in my body, like feeling water on yourself while in a shower. I could feel each muscle communicating with each nerve cell. My feet did feel like my feet, but I felt like my body existed beyond them. Sometimes It felt like I was looking at myself from a third-person view. My vision seemed to have improved significantly as well.

At first, it was overwhelming, but I got used to it. A calming sensation engulfed my body. The same sensation that I felt after I had supposedly died in that blast. After that calming sensation, I felt as if my body had always been like that. Yet I was confused as to what was happening.

Was I not a common man? How did I travel here? What was going on with my body? What was that place in my dream?

"Different?" Rohit asked.

And then the bell rang. It was time for the English period, so we had to go back to our seats. Good thing the bell rang. I am not ready to tell them about it yet.

"Well, let's see if your predictions come true," Akriti said as she quickly packed her tiffin and went to her seat.

And In came Vandana Ma'am wearing a beige Kurti and red earrings. She was quite old, I would say, but no one really knew her age. She was alright at English, but I am sure some students knew English better than her. Yet she never gave anyone proper marks and then scoffed when we complained about it. Nevertheless, she was a good person with a strong sense of justice (Except, of course, with grades; fairness seemed to disappear entirely).

"Open Chapter Eight." She shouted in that shrill voice of hers.

And as I had said before, Ma'am asked Manas to read.

"*ni* srihanni"

"It's 'Simhini' Manas!" The teacher shouted.

"Sorry, Miss." Manas apologised.

Vandana Ma'am gave him a nod to continue reading while we tried to control our laughter.

"Laali...*Lawwlittha*."

"What? Are you Bengali? It's 'Lalitha'! Sit down! Prathamesh you read!"

Prathamesh got up and tried to search for where Manas had stopped. He looked at Ma'am and then looked at Rohit. Prathamesh.

"What? Do you not know how to read?" Vandana ma'am frowned. I glanced at Rohit for a second. He was staring at Manas.

"A very good guess, right? RIGHT?", I screamed in my brain. Now they would finally start believing me for real. I do understand that it's hard to believe that someone you know is a time traveller. Why am I getting worked up for this? I'm a 21-year-old.

But then I asked myself. Was this right? Was making them believe me going to help? Am I putting them in danger by telling them?

Maybe. Maybe I shouldn't have said anything. But it was too late now. It was already done.

Next was the Sports period.

Our school did have a huge playground, but it was used mostly by the school football team, so we rarely played there. But the ground floor of our school had a huge open space.

The whole school was quadrangle-shaped. The hole in the middle of the quadrangle was quite huge, which was where we were. But since it was inside the school, it had to be tiled. The school had also converted a part of it into an indoor tennis court, which was where the girls would play.

"Ok, now Varun and Suresh, you two will be the captains. It's been twenty minutes already, children!" Our sports teacher said.

"No, I want to be the Captain!" said the prefect, Aditya.

"Dude, you are already the school prefect. Leave some leadership roles for us dude!" Said Aman.

And they kept arguing even when they made the captains, about who gets to be on whose team.

Meanwhile, Rohit was silently watching the tennis match. I moved over to Rohit.

"What do you think of the English class?" I asked him.

Rohit refused to give me a response and continued watching the match.

"Advantage!" Abhinaya screamed.

This was the first match Abhinaya was playing against Neha, who had won the first match before this one.

Abhinaya won the match. All the girls clapped, including Akriti. Our eyes met.

Akriti's face was expressionless. I smiled at her, but she quickly averted her eyes.

I looked at Rohit. He looked at me and then looked forward again. The realisation that I was not lying or playing pranks on them was too much to take in. So they were probably just waiting to see if the prediction about the tennis match would also come true. Because If it is true, then it changes their entire worldview.

I looked up at the sky.

"It sure is cloudy today," I said. Still no response from Rohit.

The second match started. Abhinaya versus Pranjal.

The ball went left and right. Pranjal was trying her best. And it did look like Abhinaya was taking it easy on Pranjal. But I don't know.

One hit on the left of the court, and the ball went to the right of Pranjal's court. Pranjal ran to hit the ball, barely managing to hit it, only for Abhinaya to take the opportunity to hit a smash.

Abhinaya had won the game again.

"What a smash Abhinaya!" Pranjal said, catching her breath. "Where did you learn to do that?"

"Oh, I went to a castle full of witches and wizards!"

"Oh, stop with that prank already!"

Really Abhinaya? What then? You'll say you use ice magic?...wait...is that how I sound when I talk about the predictions?

"There is no way you could have just guessed this. This and the English class. It's too specific." Rohit said, finally breaking his silence.
"Yeah, you believe me now, right?"

Rohit was silent for a few seconds, but then he said, "Let's wait for Notre Dame to burn."

Then the bell rang, indicating that the sports period was over. Several disappointed outcries erupted behind us.
"Next time I am making the teams, no ifs and no buts, now form a line and move back to your class." Said the Sports teacher, who then blew his whistle for the girls to get moving. Man, he should have intervened way before and made the teams.

There was one more period before the time to leave school.

At dispersal, Akriti came to our benches to talk to us.
She looked at me and said, "You really are from the future? Whatever you told us yesterday was true 100%?"
"Yes!"
"What do you think, Rohit?"
"I think...I am just confused...how is this possible?"
"Please tell me this is an extremely elaborate prank in which the whole class and everyone at the hospital are involved. I am sort of losing my sanity here, Anirudh, please."
"No, it's all true."
And then we were just staring at each other's faces.
A few moments later Akriti said, "Listen, when will you two be free this evening?"
"At around 7. Right?" Rohit said, looking at me.
"Uh, yeah."
"Then come to my house for dinner. Both of you. We will talk there. I need some time to get my thoughts together for now."

"That's fine. We will come," I said.
"Ok cool!" Akriti said with a cheerful smile, "I will make a WhatsApp group for the three of us and send you the address there!"
"Yeah, that sounds awesome!" I cheered.
"Yeah cool!" Rohit said. Then Akriti said bye and left the class.
"I guess we should head over to the bus, then?" I asked.
"yep, let's go," Rohit said.
Later that evening, after our classes, Rohit and I left for Akriti's house together.

The street lamps were up. We had entered the marigold complex and were heading towards Akriti's wing.

A group of small girls were playing hopscotch. A car coming toward us blocked my sight of the game, so I turned to look at Rohit, who was glued to his phone, trying to figure out which building was Akriti's.
"I know which one it is. No need to look."
Rohit looked at me with an annoyed expression and said, "You could have told me that long ago!"
"Yeah, sorry, I didn't know you were searching for it."
Rohit kept his phone inside his pocket.
"Was it that big of a shock? I thought you had already believed me? What happened to that, 'I believe you because you are my best friend' bullshit?"

Rohit started explaining, "Akriti and I were convinced that you were suffering from some mental disorder like schizophrenia. Although about 3 days ago, you behaved normally, there was a sudden change in your behaviour. So I did think something was wrong, but I brushed it off with the assumption that you were playing a prank, but then you fainted. Akriti and I were going to

tell the doctors everything, but since you pleaded not to, we decided to play along and see how far you can take this."
"Woah dude,"
"Yeah, I am sorry, dude. But today we thought we could find inconsistencies with your behaviour, but you ended up making us believe. A part of me is still not convinced. Your predictions for today were too specific to be just guesses or fabrications, and they even came true! But it still is a lot to take in, so I am just flowing with the river right now...how is this possible? I...I just don't understand...how can time travel be possible?"
"I wish I knew."

All of this was truly bizarre. I time-travelled into my 15-year-old body for absolutely no reason… or was there a reason? Could there be an actual world-changing reason this happened?
"Hey, that's the building," I said, looking at the concrete tower in front of us.
Marigold was built like a maze, but we found the building.

Akriti lived on the sixth floor, so we headed there using the lift.
"Welcome guys!" Akriti said with a smile as bright as a thousand suns as she opened the door to her apartment.

But suddenly a chill went down my spine. I felt as if I shouldn't be here, but I brushed it off and went inside.
Something had started. An unbelievable set of events was about to unfold.
Or so I thought.

Strange Sensations

IX

We entered her home. The eerie feeling was gone. I turned back to look outside the apartment door…and the feeling was back. Do you know how you feel if you look down at those very deep-diving pools? The pool is so deep that you can't see the bottom. That was how I was feeling. But then Akriti closed the door, and all was well. But what was it? Why did I feel that? The house itself didn't feel out of place, but I felt quite strange being there. As if someone was watching me.
"Come, sit! I am coming in a minute," Akriti said, pointing to the couch. She was wearing a yellow sundress and round, bangle-like earrings. Her hair cascaded down to her neck and ended in a beautiful curve. She was looking very pretty. Then I looked at Rohit. He was wearing cargo shorts and a multi-coloured checkered shirt with the collar button unbuttoned. The shirt hem was outside his pants and the sleeves were folded up to the elbow. And to top it off, he was wearing a sophisticated-looking watch, with a luminous dial. And then I looked at myself: just a plain red T-shirt and blue jeans. How did I become friends with such fashionable people?

Akriti went into the hallway and into the kitchen. We went on to sit on the couch. It was a set of two similar golden-coloured couches arranged in an 'L' shape. In the front of us was a 32-inch smart TV sitting on a beautiful brown cabinet which also had an intricately made sculpture of a horse on it. And then there was the rectangular coffee table in front of us. To the left of the Television cabinet was a bookshelf separated by a green potted plant and to its left was the door. The top of the bookshelf had a lot of awards, which I assumed belonged to Akriti's father. Then there was the wall to our left which had wooden wallpaper on it in contrast to the other walls, which were just light cream coloured. It had a dining table in front of it and a framed photo on the wall of Akriti with her parents. It was an old photo, for Akriti was just a child in it. The walls also had shelves with a lot of expensive-looking show-pieces on them.

Akriti came back with a tray in her hands, which she put on the coffee table and then sat on the couch to our right. The tray had cookies of several shapes and sizes. Rohit picked one up and, while pointing around the room, he said, "You sure you aren't rich, Akriti?"

Akriti smiled.

"Most of them are gifts from Grandpa. You take one of the cookies too, Anriudh! I made these!"

I took one with a surprised expression on my face.

"You can bake?" I asked. Rohit was busy munching on the cookies.

"Yeah, I have made dinner too!"

Impressed is a small word to describe what I was feeling at that moment.

"Akriti, these are the best cookies in the world!" Rohit said as he took one cookie after another.

"Hey, leave some space for dinner too! But thank you so much!"

"Akriti," I said, munching a cookie, "How are you so good at so many things?"

"My aunt taught me a lot of things. Cooking was one of them."

"I am severely impressed, Akriti!" I exclaimed.

Akriti laughed and thanked me with her hand on her chest.
"Anyway, my dad will be home by 9:30, so we have about an hour to discuss the time traveller things."
"Yeah right, let's start with you Akriti," Rohit said.
Akriti clapped her hands together and said, "Alright so..." She paused to clear her throat, "I have thought a lot about how our dear Anirudh could have predicted what he predicted today, but there is no explanation. Unless you really are a time traveller."
"I know, right? It just doesn't make any sense, but then you are a time traveller?" Rohit said.
"Yeah, that is the only explanation, mostly. And you made another prediction about Notre Dame burning right? Tell us more about that."
"Well, it's the holy week. And the cathedral is undergoing renovations. The fire broke out beneath the roof of the cathedral. By the time the structural fire was extinguished, the building's spire had collapsed, most of its roof had been destroyed, and its upper walls were severely damaged. Many works of art and religious relics were moved earlier as the fire started, but others suffered smoke damage, and some of the exterior art was damaged or destroyed. No casualties, fortunately, except 3 emergency workers who were injured."
Akriti and Rohit were looking concerned and astonished.

Then Rohit said, "I believe that you are a time traveller, but how are you able to remember all of this? You said something in school, but I didn't pay much attention."
"Yeah, ever since that headache, I feel a change in my brain. I mean, you guys saw how I solved those questions at the hospital, right? My brain feels like a search engine. All my memories are right there for me to access. The astounding thing about it is that I can remember each article I read and each video I watched very

clearly. It is so strange but at the same time here I am, having spontaneously time-travelled. Which is even more peculiar."
"That is amazing. I am just baffled, really, but I don't know…" Rohit said, slipping into a pensive state.
"But how did the fire start?" Akriti asked.
"No one truly knows, but it was mostly a short circuit. There was renovation work going on which could have increased the risk...or rather will increase a risk...er...is a risk..."
"We must warn people," Rohit said, coming out of his contemplation.
"Yeah, about this and everything you told us at the hospital," Akriti said.
"Yeah, if what you told us about the future is true, then we have to tell people about it. Yeah, not just about Notre Dame, but also about the coming pandemic and the war." Rohit blustered.
"Yeah, right," I muttered. I was not completely sure if we should be doing it at this stage, but I decided to go along anyway. What's the worst that could happen?
"Wait here for a minute," Akriti said as she got up and left the room. She came back with a laptop in her hand.
"While this is opening up, I have an idea," she said, "we could email the news channels."
"That's a good idea, but I was thinking of making a YouTube channel."
"That's a cool idea, Anirudh, but how will we grow the channel quickly?" Rohit questioned.
"Yeah, growing the channel would be problematic," Akriti said.
"How about we do both?" I said.
"Yeah! That way, we are not relying completely on the news channel to tell people about it, and at the same time we could be growing our channel with their help!" Akriti exclaimed.

"Hmmm...but how do we know that the news channel will take this seriously? Do they even check their emails in the first place?" Rohit argued.
"Well, we must try at least," Akriti said, "and here the browser started. I am creating an email account..."
"Wait!" I interrupted her. "Don't you think we should think of a way to hide our online presence? People can easily track our IP address."
"Then we should go to a cyber cafe," Rohit suggested.
"Or maybe we could use a VPN?" Akriti said.
"Oh, and I have heard about those anonymous email services," I said.
"Oh yeah, we could use that and a VPN as well," Rohit said.
"Cool, lemme set it up then, come here, " Akriti called us to sit beside her. So we sat just far enough that we weren't touching her but could still see the laptop screen.
Akriti gave us a confused look but then continued, "So I have found this website…Anirudh, tell me your email."
"aninair623@gmail.com"

The website looked like it was made in the 90s. The heading read, "The most secure anonymous email service on the internet." To use the website, you had to enter the email address of the receiver and the email would be sent. No account set-up is required. You could also set up a reply email (If the receiver replies to your anonymous mail, this email is what it would be sent to).

Ding

My phone buzzed. It was an email.

"Hello Anirudh ;)" It read. The sender profile just read Anonymous.
"Hello Akriti," I greeted Akriti while smiling ridiculously.
"Hello!" she said, also in a ridiculous fashion. We all laughed.

"Anyway, so we don't have to do any set-up? It just sends an email to whoever we want to?" Rohit asked.
"Yeah, pretty much," Akriti replied, looking at the email on my phone.
"That's pretty convenient."
"But we will still need a Gmail account for the YouTube channel," I said.
"Yeah, let's get a VPN and do that," Rohit said.
"Ok, let me search for a good free VPN."

After setting up a VPN, which was suspiciously easy to set up, we were ready to send an email.

"Should we do this at a cyber cafe?" Rohit asked.
"We are already using a VPN. Besides, we are just setting up an email. I think only for uploading a video we should go to a cyber cafe," Akriti said.

I was still unsure of whether we should be doing this. I felt that this was not going to end up well. But I guess it was really just my World War 3 PTSD talking.

"So what should the username be?"
"A real time traveller," Rohit suggested.
Akriti and I stared at him in disappointment.
"How about 'common man time traveller'?" Rohit suggested again.

We stared at him, already tired of his lamentable ideas.

"Bro, we are not writing a science fiction novel."
"Ok, how about The Reverter?" Akriti suggested.
That was a little random but had a nice ring to it, so we all agreed to use that as the username. Although its actual meaning was not related to time travel, we really liked the name.
"Now all we have to do is make the video now, and upload it tomorrow at a cyber cafe," Akriti said.

"Make the video right now?" I asked. I was getting a bad feeling about this.

"Yeah Anirudh, the sooner we do this, the better it will be," Rohit stated.

Suddenly, that strange sensation was back. I felt like my whole body was falling into an abyss. No, not just my whole body, but everything around me as well. Time had slowed down. The whole room felt like a dark place. The lights became dimmer and dimmer. Akriti's and Rohit's faces felt distorted, and then that headache again: as if I was sitting at the bottom of the Mariana Trench with a ship on my head. Time seemed to have stopped as Rohit and Akriti stopped moving; their body in awkward positions. But it was getting hard to see their distorted faces. It was getting hard to see anything in the room. The sound of the Mumbai city outside the room was slowly fading as well.

The slow darkening of the room eventually made it pitch black. Nothing was visible anymore. I couldn't hear anything either. But at least the headache was gone….well, sort of…

"Rohit?" I called out. But instead of my voice, what I heard was a reverberation of it. As if I was in a huge hall. Take the Notre Dame Cathedral and quadruple its size.

I got up from the couch and looked around. I turned around and saw a point of light ahead. I tried to touch the couch so that I could get a sense of where it was and not trip over it as I moved towards the light, but the couch had disappeared.

I was confused, but I started running towards the light anyway.

My footsteps sounded like a jackhammer because of the reverb, but my heart beat louder than my footsteps.

Soon, the reverb got smaller as the point of light transformed into a circle and its radius increased.

I could now see that I was in a cave which ended at the light source. The light source was an irregular-shaped exit out of this cave. Outside, I could see a black sky and grey ground. It was the ground that was the light source, except it was probably only reflecting the light from a larger source.

Soon I was out of the cave. I looked back into the cave, only for it to have disappeared. Fear took over me. My body was shaking.

I looked around me. Grey sand covered the landscape and stretched to the horizon, and a singular white ball of light floated in the black sky, which was so bright it would burn my eyes. And just a little ahead of me: a bus.

I immediately ran towards the bus. Maybe I could get out using the bus? It was the same bus I had seen in those dreams. As I got closer, I realised that it was the same bus I had travelled in while trying to get out of Pune before the missile strike.

The bus was empty. I walked down the walkway of the bus. Memories of people screaming from that fateful night came to me as I looked at the seats. Where was I? Why is this happening? Will I be able to go back? What does all of this mean? More and more questions ransacked my brain.

Suddenly, the door of the bus closed on its own, and the bus started moving. I ran towards the door. I desperately tried to open it, but it wouldn't budge. I moved backwards and then slammed myself on the door, but it did nothing. I repeated it again and again, but the door stood strong. The bus windows had steel rods covering them, so it was impossible to get out of them either. Besides, the bus had picked up speed. If I were to get out, I would get killed.

I frantically moved to the driver's seat to put on the brakes, but nothing happened. The bus didn't even have its engine turned on! The bus was now running a little over 100kmph and was gaining more speed. I sat in the driver's seat, terrified. 110, 115…the bus sped on.

Then I saw a stop sign directly in front of the bus. I quickly steered the bus to avoid hitting it, but then another stop sign showed itself. I turned the bus again. I was so afraid that the bus would tip over. The speed gauge showed the maximum speed, but the bus was still accelerating.

The stop signs kept appearing, their frequency increasing. I could start hearing voices as well. They were faint, but they clearly said, "Stop."

Stop? That's exactly what I tried to do! You're telling me to stop? You stop the bus!

The bus was accelerating so fast now that I could feel my body being pulled back. The signs were getting too frequent.

A blue circle which had a lot of white patches started rising on the horizon...and then I realised what that circle was.

Earth, it was the Earth, and I was probably on the moon. That huge ball of light? The sun.

The voices were becoming overbearing now as well. I felt an ever-increasing urge to cover my ears. So I left the steering wheel to close my ears, but I could still hear them.

I saw another stop sign in front of me, but before I could even touch the steering wheel, I had crashed into it.

My body flung into the windshield, breaking it. The bus had been moving so fast that it took 3 seconds for me to land on the ground. But I didn't feel any pain. No tears on my T-shirt or jeans either. I lifted myself. Even though I was physically unscathed, I was in shock. My body surged with adrenaline, though I stood perfectly still. Attempting to steady myself, I focused on calming down.

The voices had stopped as well. I looked at the bus behind me. It appeared to be in pieces. I turned around and looked at the earth again.

Even though I was on the moon, I felt no change in gravity.

"Hello! Can anybody hear me? Is someone here?" I shouted. But of course, no one was there. Was I stuck in this place forever? Probably not, but I had to get out. This was all in my head. I just needed to wake up.

And then I felt someone's footsteps right behind me. A warm hand touched my left shoulder. I was completely frozen in fear.

Then I felt a face near my ears. Some hair brushed against my ears and I could feel their breath on my cheek. Slowly the breath got closer to my ears and a very deep and guttural voice whispered, "*Or the world will end.*"

As soon as the person said that, I could no longer feel the hand or the breathing. I turned around to see that no one was there. Then I heard a huge explosion behind me.

The earth had exploded into a million pieces. An enormous piece of the earth hurdled towards me. But before it could hit me…

"What do you say, Anirudh?"

I looked around me to find myself suddenly back in Akriti's apartment. Sitting on the couch.

I looked at my watch, which read 8:45.

"Are you ok? You look a bit tense," Akriti said.

What had just happened? The world will end?

A sense of dread made my heart throb.

Was this God telling me to stop or the world will end? Should I have told them about this? Should I just tell them I was playing a prank, or that I lied about the future? Should I try to change the world? I have already changed it a significant amount by befriending Akriti. The future has already changed a little. Even though the international events would be the same, the future has changed, but is it beneficial? Images of Rohit's body emerged. He isn't going to die now. Maybe that is enough. Maybe we shouldn't try to save the world. Because it would mean the world ending? It didn't make much sense, but maybe we should just enjoy things while they last. If I try to change things, the world will turn against me. I might lose people close to me. Because changing the future would mean changing the minds of our politicians…and that place I was in a few seconds ago…also gave me signs to stop, right?

Besides, I wanted to live my high school life, right? If we were to warn people and change the future, I wouldn't be able to do that. I wouldn't fix my regrets. The only reason I told Rohit about me being from the future was that I thought it would be fun, and not because I wanted to be a 'hero'.

"Maybe we shouldn't," I said.

"What?" Rohit asked.

"Maybe we shouldn't warn the people."

"Why?"

"It took me two days to convince you two. Would the world even listen to us? I never wanted to do this. This would be too much. It will definitely be dangerous."

"We have to try Anirudh," Akriti said.

"Dude, if what you told us in the hospital is true, so many people will die! What about them? You can save them!"

"I don't think I am brave enough."

The room fell silent. After a few seconds, Rohit said, "Anirudh, I have known you for a long time now, and I know you are not a brave person. But remember, when I was in an accident, and you came rushing from your home to the site before even an ambulance could reach us?"

I remembered that. The accident happened not very far from my home, but I guess I did run. Something took over me that day, and I just knew I had to help him.

"And that time when you risked your life to save your cat?"

"Anirudh had a cat?" Akriti asked.

"Yeah, she died two years ago. My point is Anirudh, even though you are not brave, when it comes to your loved ones, you become very courageous. So let me remind you. Do you want your family to die in a nuclear blast?"

I remembered that time on the bus when I looked at the photo of my parents. I remembered all those days spent in anxiety, waiting for the wars to end. Enjoy it while it lasts? What's the point if nothing will last? How will I enjoy it if I know it's all going to end? I wanted to fix my regrets, but after what Rohit had said, I would just end up with another huge regret. Knowing that I could have saved the world, but I didn't. As stupid as it sounds, I have to be the hero that saves the world. Besides, I have already fixed one of my major regrets and made Akriti a friend. Whatever had been making me see these dreams and had been trying to tell me was definitely not a good thing. It wants the world to end; I think. I won't let that happen.

Stop or the world will end

That's what it said, right? It was clearly a threat that it would destroy the world. But I am here for a reason. People don't just travel in time spontaneously. I won't let you succeed. Whatever you are!

The strange sensation was gone. The room seemed to be getting brighter. Akriti's and Rohit's faces were no longer distorted. The slight headache remained. But I felt at peace.

"You're right, we need to warn everyone," I said.
"Now that's my Anirudh!" Rohit exclaimed.

It won't be easy, but we will change the world. Change the miserable future to a bright and cheerful one. I will revert things in the future back to how they are now. Akriti's channel name suggestion made more sense now, as random as it was.
"Alright fine then," I said. "But what would the video be like?"

We then discussed a few ideas and eventually settled on a simple audio video. The video would be blank except for a visualiser visualizing the words spoken by a text-to-speech generator.

Rohit had made this kind of video before, so he would be the one to make the video.

After a little more discussion, we settled on putting this in the video:

"Hello People of 2019, I am a common man from the year 2025.
I don't know how but I have travelled in the year 2019 from the year 2025.
Since I know what will happen in the future, I feel that I must warn everyone of the dangers that are about to come.
This video will be the first of a series of videos with predictions for the future that is my past.
My first prediction is the burning of The Notre Dame Cathedral in Paris on 15th April 2019.
Just before 18:20 Central European summer time, a fire will break out beneath the roof of the cathedral. The roof's spire will collapse along with the roof being severely damaged. There will be no casualties, except three emergency workers getting injured.
I hope you will heed my warning and act accordingly.
I will be back
Peace, The Reverter."

Rohit, Akriti and I had an expression of satisfaction on our faces, as Akriti plugged the USB drive out of the laptop. The USB drive contained the video made by Rohit.

I checked my watch. It read, "9:29." Akriti's dad would be here soon.

And that was the beginning of our journey. The journey of The Reverter. A Journey that had only just begun.

An Interrogation, And A Broken Phone

X

"Monsieur, can you please let me go now? It's been two hours," said a man dressed in a brightly coloured uniform, to a man wearing a black suit, a blue tie and sunglasses.

The man had just entered the interrogation room where the construction worker had been held. It was a dark room with a single hanging light above the chair where the worker sat. There was a table in front of him and another chair on the other side.

"Can you at least tell me how my friends are doing? You are the first person I have seen here after that officer in hours! Are you a detective or something?"

"I assure you that your friends are safe," the man said as he sat on the chair. He then folded his hands in an intimidating demeanour and put his legs on the table, but receded when he saw the worker frown.

The worker scoffed, "You're not even French."

"Yes, I am Indian, but I am currently working here. I am Officer Sam. I will ask you a few questions and you will answer them. Understood?"

That was a fake name. But Chandra deemed it necessary to use one.

The worker was not pleased, but nodded.

"I need your verbal consent."

"Oh, for God's sake! Yes!"

Chandra got up from the chair and put his hand on the table. He leaned uncomfortably close to the worker and said, "Why did you start the fire?"

"What fire?" The worker asked, looking genuinely confused.

"The cathedral."

"Preposterous! Do you think I'm an Arsonist? I want a lawyer! Get me one! Right now!"

Chandra stepped back and started walking around the chair.

"Where were you when the fire started?"

"That's none of your business! Just get me a lawyer, why won't you?"

"LSD is a fine drug, ain't it?"

The worker went completely silent. Chandra stopped walking and put his hands on the table again.

"Where were you when the fire started?"

"I swear to you! I didn't start the fire! You imbecile!"

"That was not my question!" Chandra bellowed and slammed the table loudly.

The worker flinched.

"I was with my mistress! Please..."

He had started sobbing softly.

"Ah, shameless fellow. You're married, aren't you?"

"Please don't tell my wife."

Chandra grabbed him by his shirt and pinned him to the wall. In a very intimidating and angry voice, he asked, "I am not going to ask you again. Where were you when the fire started?"

Suddenly, the door to the room burst open.

A lady wearing a black suit and a blue shirt walked in.

"Qui es-tu?" She said with a shocked expression on her face.

Chandra quickly left the worker and sprinted towards the door. He tackled the woman and ran out.

"There is a man! We have an intruder! Black suit and sunglasses!" She shouted in French into her transponder as she tried to get up.

Alarms started ringing.

"Quick Chandra!" A man shouted on Chandra's transponder. He increased his pace.

He was just about to reach the exit when he saw a police officer.

"Arrêt!" the officer shouted with his gun pointed at him. Chandra stopped. The exit was right behind the officer.

"Hands up!" The officer commanded in French.

Chandra quickly took out his gun and pointed it at the officer.

The officer immediately spoke into his transponder, "Need backup at the North exit!"

Just as Chandra was about to pull the trigger, the exit door shattered. A man dressed in the same manner as Chandra emerged out of it and hit the officer on his head with a fire extinguisher. The officer immediately dropped to the ground.

"Let's go!" He motioned to Chandra. They sprinted out of the precinct.

"I thought you were supposed to keep the woman occupied?"

"Yeah, she got suspicious. We'll talk about it later. Now move it! And were you just about to shoot that officer?!"

Chandra shrugged and hopped over the wall of the police precinct. Shekhar followed. They climbed on their bikes. The engines growled as they rode off onto the streets of Paris.

They weren't too far from the precinct when they caught the attention of two police cars.

"Damn!" said Shekhar, "Chandra! Lose them and then get to the Airport!"

Chandra and Shekhar split up.

The police cars followed them.

Chandra sped on the road and dodged one vehicle after another.

The way to the airport was long and there were too many cars. But he spotted an alley to his right. It was too narrow for the police cars but large enough for him. So he went inside and ditched the bike there.

He immediately ran across it and got in a taxi before the police could find a way around the alley.

"To the Airport, please! I will miss my flight!" Now there was no way the police could catch him in time. He hoped that Shekhar had made it as well.

About 15 minutes later, he arrived at the airport. And Shekhar was standing alongside their Paris correspondent.

"Here are your tickets."

"Thank you, Madhavan sir."

"Don't thank me yet, get on the flight and leave! The police are smart enough to figure out that you are here, and will be here soon!"

"Yes sir, but weren't we supposed to go to Mumbai? Why have you given us tickets for Delhi?"

"The people from the headquarters aren't exactly happy with you…Now, go!"

"Yes, sir."

Chandra and Shekhar swiftly made their way to their terminal, aiming to catch their flight. Before the police could intervene, the flight had already departed with them on board.

They felt relieved that they weren't caught. However, they didn't get the information they wanted, and that was a huge let-down.

"Please tell me he was the one involved. You didn't torture him, did you?"

"No, just threatened him, but he probably wasn't involved. I would have liked more time with him if only you didn't screw up."

"Oh, come on, mister crybaby. Honestly, the success of this whole operation of yours seemed dubious to me right from the start."

"Look, if I am right about this, then we might just uncover the greatest conspiracy in the history of mankind."

"Might? Your whole theory is based on a viral YouTube video uploaded on a channel made 6 days ago! That is very well a fake video that coincidently got things right. That's it!"

"Nothing is ever a coincidence and no, it's not just that…if only the useless headquarters people would have given me more resources…"

"Yeah, after what you did on our last mission? You know you were about to shoot that police officer today as well! How many more innocent people will die because of you? Chandra, this is our last mission together."

Shekhar immediately took out his headphones and blindfold and tried to doze off; Chandra stared at the beautiful Paris city outside his window.

But he was angry. No matter which way you see this mission was a complete failure. He thought of how, if he were a giant, he could just crush the Eiffel Tower beneath his shoes. He brushed off the thought and tried to sleep as well. He will have his chance to spew his anger properly…or so he thought. Chandra was particularly proud of his expertise, and wouldn't let anyone or anything come in his way.

After landing in Delhi, they were escorted to the NIA headquarters.

In all of his career, Chandra always felt that he never got what he rightfully deserved. Even though he had helped stop countless terrorist attacks, no one ever took him seriously. Not even his closest friend, whom he called his friend, but was just his partner at work. But what he had discovered recently would change everything. He was sure of it.

"Ah, Officer Chandra. Back from the moon, eh?"

Chandra and Shekhar were now standing in front of the security council. The chairman started speaking with Chandra. It was a rectangular room with an oval-shaped table in the middle. The chairman was sitting at the end.

"Chandra, you and your partner almost got caught. And although we told you not to go ahead with the plan, you still did anyway. This is not acceptable at all!"

"I am sorry, sir. All I ever wanted was to save our nation and possibly the world from this terrorist organisation."

"A terrorist organisation, that doesn't exist."

"How can a cathedral just spontaneously start burning?"

"That is your argument?" said someone in the council.

"No, this," Chandra said, placing a USB drive on the chairman's desk, "is my argument."

The chairman stared at him and then at the USB drive. Finally, he gestured to the peon to bring in the projector. The lights were dimmed, the USB drive was connected to the computer, and the projector was turned on.

Hundreds of charts and screenshots of Excel sheets popped up. After selecting a few of them, Chandra started speaking.

"On 5th April, a series of radio bursts of varying frequencies was observed in the city of Mumbai. These are not normal radio wave frequencies that are used on FM or AM radio. But either much higher or much lower. Their range doesn't fall under telecommunication either, except they could still be used for communication in a certain way. It was not possible to determine their origin, but these were definitely being used for communication.

"And what makes you say that?" said some from the council.

"They all followed the same modulations. Very similar and subtle changes in frequency and amplitude. Moreover, since 5th April they have been happening very frequently. And they were never observed before. On and before the upload date of the YouTube video, from the channel 'The Reverter' on which the uploader claims to be a time traveller, the observations increased. A similar increase was noticed yesterday when Notre Dame burned as well and in several parts of the world, however, they seemed to be more in number in Mumbai. Now these outbursts have been emitted from all over the city. My first thought was that it could be related to a faulty power supply…but after contacting some authorities, I realised that was not the case. And the same problem occurring all over the world at the same time is unrealistic. But this is not even the most interesting thing. The most interesting thing is this observation. "

Chandra magnified one of the charts. It showed two maps of India side by side. There were various spikes of different colours all over it,

"This is an overall EMF observation chart across India. The left one is from before 5th April and the right one is from on 5th April."

Confused chattering could be heard in the room.

The chart showed a completely abnormal spike across Mumbai and its surrounding areas, including Thane, Vasai, Virar, Nashik and Pune. Even in places where there should have been nothing but forests.

"What do you propose is happening?" someone from the council questioned.

"I think there is a massive worldwide terrorist organisation operating out of Mumbai. And I don't think these are terrorists originating from any religious group. They seem to be highly coordinated and also seem to have advanced technology."

"This is certainly worth looking into. Although the correlation between this and that YouTube channel is circumstantial at best, we will look into it. But are you sure about this?" said the chairman.

"Have I ever been wrong before?"

"You have been," Shekhar said.

"Did anything come off your musings in Paris?" the chairman asked.

"No sir."

"How many views does this…the reverter have?"

"About 2 million now, sir, and rising."

The chairman nodded while staring at the graphs. Perhaps this was all too much to be believable.

"You both can go for now. The council will discuss this and we will notify you."

"Thank you, sir."

They were almost out of the room when the chairman stopped them and said, "And If you are reluctant to follow orders again, you will be relieved of your duty."

"It won't happen again sir,"

"Good."

"Oh, you will beg me to carry out your operations," Chandra thought to himself as he walked out.

After roaming around for a while, Chandra went to sit in the lobby and called his family. It was well beyond closing time, so there was no one in the lobby. His 5-year-old daughter picked up the call.

"Hey, daddy! It's been such a long time since you called!"

"Yeah, I know, sweetie. You know how daddy is busy catching bad guys!"

"You are a superhero, daddy!"

"Aww, thank you, darling! Where's your mom?"

"Mom says she doesn't want to talk to you."

"How can she…Myra give your mom the phone?"

"What is it, Chandra?" An older female voice was on the phone.

"Why did you say that to Myra?"

"When are you coming home?"

Chandra didn't know what to say.

"Don't call us again if you don't want to be with us."

"Oh, come on! Hello Aisha, hello I…"

Aisha had cut the phone. Chandra squeezed the phone and then threw it across the room in anger. The phone hit the wall and fell to the ground with a loud thud and a shattering sound.

"Chandra!" Shekhar was standing at the entrance. Chandra got up and tried to calm himself down. Shekhar stared at the broken phone and then gave a confused look at Chandra.

"What?" Chandra asked.

"Pack up, we're going to Mumbai."

A wide grin filled Chandra's face.

"Time to catch some bad guys," he said. His eyes filled with the fire of determination and sheer ambition.

A Red Sky

XI

"Where is Akriti? It's already 5:22! The movie starts at 5:30!" Rohit asked.
"Don't worry, she will be here soon."
"I think I need to call her. She probably forgot that she needs to be here."

Rohit removed the phone from his pocket and called Akriti. She picked up the phone and shouted, "I'm coming in a minute!" And immediately hung up.
"I guess she's coming?" Rohit said, rubbing his ear to soothe the pain of Akriti's verbal assault through the phone.

It was the 26th of April. We were at the cinema hall to watch the premiere of The Avengers: Endgame. But it was mainly a cover for us to secretly discuss our next video, or at least that's why I had agreed to go and watch the movie.

Starting with just 103 views before the fire on 15th April, the first video had gained 4 million views, and the views were increasing along with our subscriber count. We no longer needed the TV channels and could operate using the YouTube channel. Not everyone believed us, but enough people were following this for the world to be interested. Now, all we had to do was wait for Akriti to arrive.

But then I remembered something I had to talk about with Rohit; About Akriti. I liked her, but I didn't know what I should do with my feelings. Now felt like a good time to talk about it with Rohit, as no one we knew was around in the lobby of the cinema hall.

"So…Rohit?"
"Yeah?"
"I wanted to talk to you about Akriti."
"I'm listening," he said, his eyes wide with curiosity.
"I…like her."

Rohit's face instantly went into shock. After scratching his head a bit, he blurted out, "Woah! OMG, dude! Since when?"
"Since 9th standard."
"That is…wow! I mean, I had a feeling you did—"
"But you know the problem is that technically I am a 21-year-old?"
"Oh yeah, I didn't think about that. But is that really a problem?"
"Doesn't that make me a paedophile?"
Rohit laughed.
"I wouldn't say that, dude. When you started liking her, you were her age, right? Although I can't believe you didn't find anyone else all those years, I won't call you a paedophile. Yes, if you were 40 years old and then travelled back in time. Yeah, you need to move on, Grandpa. But you're not. Your body right now is 15 years old anyway! So don't worry too much about it. But she does know that you are from the future. My point is that liking her isn't a problem, but she might not like you romantically. 7 years is a huge gap like you said."
"Ok, I guess. You know in my future past I never managed to find the courage to talk to her and now I am her friend. I mean, can you believe that she actually lived this close to me? I will get plenty of chances to impress her."
"Look, don't actively try to impress her or anything. She doesn't seem to be that kind of girl. For now, just be a good friend. I'll tell

you if you need to do something. And also she is smart. She will probably figure it out herself."

"That I like her?"

"That you like her. But you are a decent guy, so the worst-case scenario is that she friend-zones you. At Least you are not like me."

Rohit used to be a playboy. In 9th standard, he had 3 girl-friends: one at school, one at tuition and one online. They didn't do anything obscene besides hugging (if you consider that ob-scene), but he eventually got caught and his 'reputation' went down, so no girl wanted to be with him after that.

For me, it doesn't matter if she isn't my 'girlfriend', I Just want to be with her. And if that is as a friend, I am absolutely fine with it. Because love is a flower that you must let grow. At the same time, you shouldn't want to be stuck in the friend zone. Not that I know how to get out of it since I never even got into the friend zone.

"It's been five minutes now. Where is she? The movie will start!" Rohit complained.

Soon we saw an auto-rickshaw across the turn and it came towards us. But it didn't stop. It wasn't her.

We both were getting frustrated. Where was she?

"Boo!"

Akriti had somehow sneaked behind us and startled us.

"My God Akriti!" Rohit blustered. Akriti was giggling.

"Where were you?" I asked. But seeing as to how heavily she had her make-up on today, I think I didn't need to ask that.

"Sorry guys, let's not waste more time now. Let's go inside," she said.

We sat in the theatre waiting for the movie to start. I had watched this movie too many times. And with my super memory,

I could practically rewatch it in my head…but it was too boring now. It was extremely irritating to watch this movie again.

A few kids were singing The Avengers Theme song loudly. It reminded me of the first time I watched the film with Rohit.

I sighed and said, "You know, I have already watched this movie many times."

Akriti had a look of horror on her face.

"Oh no," she said.

Rohit started laughing at her weird expression, to which Akriti punched Rohit's shoulder.

"Don't worry, I am not going to give any spoilers."

Akriti sighed relief. What's wrong with her today? She had been acting quite strange since we went viral on YouTube. She had become a little less talkative as well. Everything she says and the way she behaves feels like an act. But to be honest, it kind of felt like that from the very beginning.

The movie started, and I tried to watch it, but I fell asleep halfway through. Yes, it was that boring for me. It's not that I hate the movie, but the sheer number of times Sarvesh made me watch this movie, has made me want to go to Marvel Studios and every place where the movie exists, and destroy it.

Rohit woke me up at the end of the movie and we went to sit in the McDonald's restaurant.

"Was it really that boring for you?" He asked.

"You try watching the same movie 500 times."

"Anyway, let's discuss our next video, shall we?"

"Yes," I said.

"So what's your next prediction, Anirudh?" Akriti asked.

I took a trip down the galaxy of my memory—which had become a very fast process now—and said, "The cyclone 'Fani', an extremely severe cyclone will make landfall in Odisha on 3rd May. It will be the worst storm in Odisha since the 1999 Odisha cyclone. Approximately 72 people were killed with 8.85 billion dollars, that is about 619 billion rupees."

"Oh, My God!" Rohit screeched.

Akriti was also in shock but was being her new, nonchalant self.

"Well, I am going to go home and make the video immediately," Rohit said.

"Chill, eat for now. I am going to the washroom," Akriti said as she got up and went away.

"But we must evacuate everyone from the coasts!"

"Chill Rohit, we will get the video up by tomorrow."

Our order was up, so we went to get it. Akriti came back at almost the same time.

The cyclone was not the worst thing that was about to happen in the future. Many more people, in fact, the entirety of humanity, along with several other species, were facing extinction.

We started eating. I was having a McDonald's burger after a very long time. Because of the war, these things were either completely not available or extremely overpriced. McDonald's was not the only franchise that faced this issue.

The cool air of the restaurant felt soothing, and the smell of coffee tantalised me to go and drink a whole drum's worth of coffee. These are the small things that we are very lucky and privileged to enjoy and things we often take for granted.

Suddenly, I felt that someone was watching me. I looked around, but nothing seemed out of the ordinary. This was the same feeling I had before entering Akriti's apartment before that headache took me to the hospital and the moon. I grew anxious as I

was either going to that same place again, or something incredibly bad was about to happen.
"Are you ok Anirudh?" Rohit asked.

I just stared at him, my hands frozen with the burger in them. Sweat dripped down my cheeks, my heartbeat got faster. The weight of the whole world seemed to be on my head, and as if the weight was too much, everything around me started to shake.
"It's an earthquake!" someone screamed.
Everybody started screaming and flitted out of the restaurant.

"Anirudh, let's go!" Rohit screamed. But I was too scared to move. People's screams could still be heard. Every inch of my body was telling me something was very wrong. But I was too scared to do anything. Rohit tried to yank me off the chair, and Akriti helped him. But slowly, the sound of screaming was replaced with silence. My sight grew dim, and I fainted. Out of fear, or because of otherworldly forces? I didn't know. But what I did know was that there was nothing in God's holy hair that could tell me that this was good. An earthquake in Mumbai suggested that something was very wrong.

I woke up in a white place. White all around. I couldn't even see my shadow. I was standing on something, but there seemed to be no ground. As if someone had dropped you into a bucket full of extremely thin white paint and backlit the bucket.

And I was still very frightened.

But then I heard a female voice. The same voice I had heard on the moon. But this time, the voice had a calming effect on my mind.

"I am dying. He is coming. You must race. But there is hope. This world, only you can save. Rage and race. Rage and race. Rage and race."

Then I felt weightless. Everything went dark, and I was back in our world. I slowly gained my senses.

"Anirudh! Are you ok?"

I looked at Rohit on my left.

"Say something Anirudh!" Akriti screamed to my right.

We were on the streets now, just outside McDonald's. It was full of people. Cars honked loudly, police sirens buzzed all around. I was sitting on the sidewalk along with Rohit and Akriti.

"I am fine," I said.

"Anirudh. Is there something you are not telling us?" Akriti asked.

I stared at her solicitous face. She stared back. I turned and looked towards Rohit, who was also staring at me with concern. I then looked at the sky.
But looking at the sky surprised me. I got up.

"Do y'all see that?" I asked them. They both got up and looked at the night sky.
"See what?" Rohit asked.

The sky was red. As if there was a huge fire circling the whole of Mumbai. The sky should have been black, but it was red.
"The sky is red!" I screamed. A few people looked at us. It was about 9 pm right now. The sky shouldn't be red. Why was it red?
"Let's go to your house, Anirudh," Rohit said.
"No, mine," Akriti said.

"Alright, anyone's house, let's just go!" Rohit shouted in frustration.

He is coming, you must race.

Who was coming? Why was the night sky red? Why couldn't anyone but me see it? Where should I run to? Why did that voice have to be so vague? What was that voice? And why was it dying?

I was slowly becoming less frightened as we moved ahead towards Akriti's house. The sky, however, remained red. It was the same sky as the one I saw in my first and second dreams. I remembered that thing that fell on me in the first dream. Was this what that female voice was talking about?

If I think about it, the place I went to during the first dream and the one when I fainted after the test differed from the one I had at Akriti's house and the restaurant. There was also this weird sense of clarity that I had been feeling ever since I woke up on the street. This feeling of clarity and calmness was the thing that was quenching my fear. These dreams meant something. Something related to me travelling back to 2019.

Rohit's phone rang. It was from his parents. He talked with them for a while and assured them that he was fine and would be coming home soon. Then my phone rang and soon after that Akriti's phone did too. We unanimously decided to talk at the gate of Akriti's housing complex and then leave for our homes. I explained to them everything that had happened in my so-called dreams when we reached the gate. People were starting to go back home as the police suggested, except a few who were still out on the streets, but I don't think anyone would pay attention to three teenagers talking 'nonsense' right after an earthquake.

"And you didn't think of telling us?!" Rohit shouted. Akriti was just silently staring at me.

"You all were already thinking that I was crazy, saying this would have been like shooting my self in the foot!"
"What about *after* we started believing you?"
"I was too scared to talk about it."
"Too scared?! Seriously Anirudh? Here I am just absolutely worried about you fainting all the time and…it's not just that Anriudh…Do you realise how incredibly crazy everything is? You time travelled! You are seeing a red sky that we don't! And now there are these dreams that…" Rohit stopped speaking, putting his hands on his hips and stared at the ground indignantly.
"I'm sorry," I said. Rohit looked up and sighed.
"It's just a lot to take in, and you, not telling us everything, is the worst thing," he said.
"I understand. I won't have any secrets from now on."

Then Akriti finally spoke, "Whatever is happening, our goal is still the same: Save the world from a nuclear disaster. So we will continue to make the videos for now and think about what these dreams mean. Let's just go and talk about it tomorrow. Anirudh, you go home and send Rohit what you want to say, then Rohit will make the video and give it to me tomorrow. I will upload it as I go to the hospital in the evening."
"Should we even make a video? Because I think our video going viral is the cause of all this," Rohit.
"For now, let's make the video and we will discuss tomorrow whether we should upload it or not."

At home, we watched the news, where they said that as the earthquake lasted only for 10 seconds, there was no damage except for a few things falling from shelves in people's homes. The people were told to stay alert for the time being.

No one was going to go to sleep that night.

At 10:06 pm the news channels revealed that the National Centre for Seismology and the Indian Meteorological Department had declared no tsunami warning and that the earthquake was only a magnitude four on the Richter scale, but the epicentre was at a distance of 100km below Mumbai, and it was likely because of a natural gas pressure release. This was a bit concerning, but I knew that it was not the real reason for the earthquake, because when I looked outside my window, the sky was still red.

The City of Dreams

XII

As Chandra stepped out of his car, the vibrant blue of the sky shimmered in its reflection. Shekhar followed, glancing at the mesmerising Taj Hotel and The Gateway of India behind him. A vast flock of pigeons took flight before it, painting the sky with the hues of their purple-grey feathers.

"And why are they here?" Chandra asked Shekhar.

"Well, Mr Roy said that we need a vast network If we want to figure out who these people are," Shekhar said.

"That does make sense."

"And also to keep you at bay."

Chandra stopped walking and glared at Shekhar, who ignored him and kept walking towards the hotel gate.

"Hurry up! You don't want to be late for the meeting, Chandra!" He shouted without looking back.

The pigeons had now flown over to the top of the Taj hotel and were probably searching for a car to defecate on.

Soon, Chandra and Shekhar reached the conference room of the hotel. The grand hotel and its history were the reason Chandra wanted to become an NIA officer. It was also the reason the NIA was created.

As Chandra and Shekhar entered, loud chatter filled the conference room; silenced by the gesture of the chairman. The conference room was quite big, with a golden chandelier in the middle. On an oval, round table in the middle of the room sat about 6 people. But there was one who Chandra didn't recognise. There was also a small stage next to a screen a few feet from the table.

Chandra was surprised to see the chairman. Normally, he wouldn't be present for such meetings—It is a security issue, and he has other administrative tasks to do—But his presence meant that the N.I.A. was finally taking him seriously. His hard work would be paid off, and he would get the recognition he deserves.

"Good Morning sir," Shekhar said.

"Good Morning Chandra and Shekhar."

"Good morning sir," Chandra blurted, having forgotten to greet the chairman in his vanity.

"I assume that you have some things to tell us and you know that RAW is here as well."

"Yes, sir."

"Well Then! Go ahead."

Chandra moved to the stage while Shekhar plugged in Chandra's laptop to the projector. He carefully adjusted his tie and waited for Shekhar to get the graphics running. The screen flashed, and he was ready to begin.

"Everyone knows the reverter's prediction for the fire and the cyclone has been correct. However, they could not predict an event as big as an earthquake in Mumbai. Since the cause of the earthquake has still not been accurately determined, it could be something that the group did. Maybe something went wrong with their equipment, something they didn't think would happen; they couldn't include it on their YouTube channel even though they did say that the earthquake didn't happen in their timeline. This has decreased their views significantly. If you read my report, you know these people are probably using incredibly advanced communication technology and they seem to operate through Mumbai.

I believe this reverter group is an organisation of highly intelligent individuals, and they are planning something big. And if they are the reason for the earthquake's occurrence...then whatever they are planning will have a significant effect."
Then a man wearing a suit stood up and started speaking, "Good morning, I am Prakash Srivastava, from RAW. I won't tell you my rank for security reasons, but I am one of the people acting as a spokesperson for RAW."
It seemed that RAW maintained a superior system of security (Or so Chandra thought). Having introduced himself, Prakash continued, "So far, the proofs that you have submitted do seem to suggest that there is a stark difference between them and other terrorist groups that the NIA has been investigating. Their warning about the cyclone did save some lives, and they haven't done anything that a terrorist organization would do, but they must have had some other motives. Good or bad, we must understand who they are and what they want. In the end, it is also possible that reality could be different from what we have assumed. Nevertheless, it is something to be looked into thoroughly. Now, RAW has tried to identify them using the IP addresses they could have used for uploading the video, but they seem to be using VPNs. However, we could pinpoint a certain area using the HTTP requests made on the upload dates, tracing their VPN to a specific set of servers—they are probably using a very cheap VPN service–and through the EMF data provided by Mr Chandra."
"That is amazing work!" Chandra said.
"It is the RAW, after all," the chairman said. Chandra nodded with a smile.

Prakash gave Shekhar a pen drive. It contained a map of a normal neighbourhood in Mumbai, with a red circle surrounding it.

"Now, we can't say which building they could be operating from or whether they are even here, but we do have a trainee agent working in the Chamunda hospital. We have told the agent to report to us if anything unusual happens. If anything, we could locate their technology if it exists here."
"Then we must send in more of our agents there, alert the police for suspicious activities, and monitor the movement of goods in and out of this neighbourhood," Chandra said.
"Hold your horses," said an old man with a brown cane in his hand. "All the intelligence we have gathered is based primarily on a random YouTube channel, which could simply be a few talented teenagers having fun. And those EMF fluctuations could simply be a coincidence don't you think? The intel RAW has gathered could be related to anything. In my opinion, this investigation is a waste of resources."

Chatter filled the room again.

"Silence!" the chairman said. "I think we are past the point of believing that this is just a coincidence. I do agree that reality could be far from what we think, but there is no doubt that something fishy is going on."
"I am sorry, sir, but this is just hard to believe," the old man said. "I, for one, can't believe Chandra's intuition and flawed intellect."

That blew Chandra's fuse, and he spoke in a rather loud voice, "Mr Venkateshwar, what do you think is more plausible, a time traveller? Or an organisation coordinating on an international level? Or are some teenagers travelling to Paris and burning a cathedral for fun? Who gave you this job, Mr Venkateshwar? Were they drunk?"

"Chandra! You are crossing your limit!" The Chairman blared.

"Sorry, sir. But Mr Venkateshwar has an illegitimate and illogical hatred for me. I think his narrow-mindedness would keep us from moving forward. It *is obstructing* us at this moment."
"Mr Venkateshwar, please control yourself. And Chandra, I don't want to hear such insolence from you again."
"Sorry, Sir."
"I am sorry sir, but I refuse to work with Chandra. I request you put me off this investigation," the old man said.

An awkward silence filled the room.

After a few seconds, the chairman spoke. "You may leave Mr Venkateshwara."

Suddenly, the Door to the conference room burst open, and a man hurried in towards the chairman. He spoke something in the chairman's ears, and the chairman's eyes widened for a second.

Calmly, the chairman asked to turn on the news. The projector screen was now displaying a live broadcast from a news channel.
"Breaking news! The famed time traveller has uploaded another video and it will shock you! Here is the video:"

"Hello people of 2019, This is the Reverter and my next prediction is for 12th May, 3 days from now.
4 commercial ships: two Saudi Aramco oil tankers, Almarzoqah and Amjad, the UAE flagged A.Michel, and the Norwegian Andrea Victory, are damaged while anchored near Fujairah, in the Gulf of Oman.
The US will blame Iran. This is one of the things that will fuel World War 3 in 2024.
This attack must be stopped. I will give more details about World War 3 in a future video which will be purely about the coming

dangers. All I can do is warn everyone. I hope you will heed my warning and monitor those ships.

Peace, The Reverter."

More than the attack, the words 'World War 3' and 'coming dangers' plagued Chandra's mind. He had forgotten completely about his dispute with Mr Venkateshwar.

"No human can remember things from seven years ago in such great detail. This is planned. It's almost as if they are telling us they will attack these ships!" said a woman sitting beside the old man. She was Mrs Subramaniyam. She handled the Kashmir Project for the NIA.

"It does seem like it, doesn't it?" Chandra said.

"I think we will need international help to solve this. Chandra, can you look at the EMF readings right now?" the chairman said.

"Yes sir."

Chandra swiftly went towards his laptop. After loading up the data, and converting it into human-readable graphs (using an algorithm that he built himself), Chandra projected the charts onto the screen.

The charts clearly showed a rapid increase in EMFs around Mumbai and the port of Fujairah.

"I think the videos are a form of communication and the EMFs are a form of confirmation," Shekhar said.

"But then why would they create it in a way that it goes viral? And why share it on social media accounts?" said the old man.

"That is something that we will have to figure out," said Shekhar.

"That is an interesting proposition though, Mr Shekhar, and don't worry about international agencies. RAW will take care of it," said Mr Prakash.

Chandra was silently staring at the charts. His mind was fixated on the mention of the words 'World War 3'.
"They must have purposefully used a cheap VPN so that anyone trying to find them would focus their resources on a possibly false location," Chandra thought. He felt that something was very wrong with this. His gut feelings were screaming.
Suddenly, Chandra felt an extremely strange sensation. Something that he had never felt before. A peculiar combination of dread and sadness. The lights in the room started to dim for Chandra until everything went dark. But immediately the room was illuminated with red lights, making everything look bloodied and macabre.
He looked around, only to find that no one was moving. The cup of tea in the chairman's hand was about to splatter its contents into his lap as it had started to fall out of his hands, except that it was as still as a portrait.
The red lights were increasing their brightness linearly with the temperature of the room.
Chandra was petrified. His eyes were wide and his blood was cold.
"Must capture the reverter. Must kill him," a very deep voice reverberated in the room. Chandra's heart throbbed. He looked around to locate the source, but the terrible atmosphere of the room stopped him from moving. He had turned and was frozen in fear.

"Ahhh!" the chairman screamed as the tea fell onto his pants. Everyone rushed to look at the chairman.

"Everything is normal now?" Chandra said softly, still scared and confused. If everyone could see and hear what Chandra had, they wouldn't immediately rush towards the chairman but would be as dazed as Chandra.

"Don't just stand there all scared! Go bring a towel, Chandra!" Shekhar said.

Chandra nodded and sprinted out of the room.

He was still extremely confused. What had just happened? What was the voice? Why did it want to kill the reverter? And was the reverter a single person?

Chandra stared at himself in the mirror of the bathroom. Wondering about it all.

The mirror suddenly turned red, and Chandra could hear the voice in his head, "*I will help you save the world.*"

***

After that conference, there were several meetings on different days to coordinate the investigation between NIA and RAW. Task Forces were made and money was spent.
But nothing happened on the day of the Gulf of Oman incident. The Gulf of Oman incident never occurred.
A few days later, a new video appeared on the channel in which the reverter thanked the 'people of 2019' for preventing the Gulf of Oman incident. But that video had even fewer views than usual.

There were more videos released by the Reverter in June and July regarding predictions for cricket matches. These videos gained a lot of views, but people mostly accused the matches of being fixed.

Then in August, the Reverter released a long video which described in detail the 'coming dangers' of World War 3 and the pandemic, but that video had even fewer views than the thank you video. It seemed that people were losing interest in the reverter. "Just another fool pretending to be a time traveller for views," they said.

But there was someone who hadn't lost any interest. Someone who watched every second and every frame of the videos carefully. Someone who had been having nightmares of a Mumbai filled with fire and deep voices. Voices that screamed that he needed to catch the Reverter. Chandra was showing a maniac level of interest in the investigation.

Others thought that it was normal for 'Mad Chandra', but Shekhar knew that something was wrong.

Chandra had started lashing out at his juniors. Something that he had never done before.

"Chandra, are you ok?"

Chandra stared at him for a few seconds and then spoke, "Everything is normal, Shekhar. Where is the data I asked for?"

"It's being processed."

"You didn't put it on parallel processing?"

"No."

Chandra's face immediately turned infuriated.

"Then go do it now!" he shouted.

Shekhar stared at him in disgust for a few seconds.

"What Shekhar?!" Chandra shouted.

"Chandra, you need to take a break from this investigation. I will ask to be assigned somewhere else. Goodbye."

And Shekhar left without turning back.

For a moment, Chandra felt remorse for lashing out at Shekhar. But the deep voices took over his brain.

"Don't you all have work to do!?" Chandra screamed at everyone watching. Everyone scuffled and went back to their work.

The red sky was getting darker.

Stunned and Petrified

XIII

"It's been a week, Anirudh," Rohit said in a gloomy voice.
It was the 19th of November. 3 months had passed since the major reveal video came out. Covid-19 was starting to emerge but of course, no one but a few people knew that it was. Although I had warned everyone about a major pandemic and a major war in the future, pathetically few people believed us. People lost interest simply because we couldn't predict an earthquake and had effectively prevented the Gulf of Oman incident.

The pandemic, however, was the least of my concerns.

At 10 in the morning, amidst the birds' cheerful chirping and their flights in search of food for their young, while cars gleamed under the sunlight, trapped in the cacophony of traffic, I glanced out of my classroom window. Despite everything else shining in the daylight, the sky appeared ominously black. It had progressively gotten darker since the earthquake and was now completely black. And I felt that it was getting even darker day by day.

I still had very little knowledge of why the sky was so dark, but as if this menacing darkness wasn't enough, we had another problem.

Akriti had disappeared. It had been a week, and we were worried.

She had not come to school for a week. She wasn't picking up calls or seeing our text messages. There was no one in her house as well. We had gone there several times in the past three days.

We had even gone to the hospital, but there was no sign of her. We were now getting very worried about her. The staff said that they hadn't seen her for the past two weeks either.

Since the earthquake, Akriti had been having less and less contact with us. It was always, "Oh I have homework," or "I have some work at the hospital." Very rarely did she spend time with us. And after the major reveal video, the more we tried to engage her, the more she went away.

She never disappeared in my future past. Her disappearance had something directly to do with me. Or was it because of 'him'? The 'him' I am supposed to run from? The 'him' that the female voice warned me about? The images of the exploding earth flashed before my eyes again. Where was Akriti?

I looked out the window again. The black sky now filled my heart with dread. Where was Akriti? Really, where was she?

"Should we go to her dad's clinic?" I asked.

"That is a good idea. Why did we not think of that?" Rohit said, with his eyes enlarged.

"Because we don't know where it is."

"Yeah, we never asked her."

But then it hit me.

"I do know where it is!"

"How? Anirudh, she never told us."

"She did! Remember, on 7th September after lunch, when we asked Akriti to come to talk about the channel?"

"We asked her to talk about the channel a million times now. No, I don't remember that. No human being can possibly remember that."

"She told us that she had to go to Silver Road."
"And how does that connect to the location of her dad's clinic?"
"I asked her why, and she told me that she had to visit her dad's clinic."
Rohit's eyes enlarged again.
"Wait, I do remember! Let's go there right after school. We'll tell the bus driver to let us off earlier at Rajni Circle," He said.
"Perfect."

I looked at the sky again. Dread now turned to hope. Small but powerful hope.

But I don't get it. When everything appeared so shiny and bright, why did the sky specifically look like God decided to open up his holy computer, and use a fill bucket in Microsoft Paint to make the sky black?

But then the answer was simple: 'him'

He is coming, you must run.

The line repeated in my head. But the sky would be black wherever I go. Where would I run off to?

This was quite frustrating. I want to do something about it. But I don't know what. The voice clearly said I am the only one who can save the world, but I didn't have a single clue. And Akriti's week-long disappearance wasn't helping either.

Nevertheless, after school, we did exactly what we planned. We were going to find her.
"There's only one clinic on Silver Road and it's beside the only chemist shop," Rohit said.

Silver Road was nothing special.

The sidewalk was flanked by trees, casting shadows that further diminished the already scarce sunlight, courtesy of the surrounding buildings. The streets seemed narrower because of cars lining the curbs. However, it was the yellow residential buildings adorned with white lines of plaster used to fill cracks that truly defined the area—a distinctive mark of its residential character.

A 6ft long, yellow-coloured wall and the sidewalks separated the buildings and the street. The trees were beautiful; they had yellow flowers on them during spring which fell like cherry blossoms. But now, in November, they were all starting to shed their leaves, waiting for the winter to come and pass.

After walking past the gates of a few buildings, we came across a small two-story building with a few photocopy shops and a chemist on the ground floor. And beside the chemist was a staircase that led to the clinic.

"Sri Sai clinic," a board read on a wall above the entrance to the stairs.

Immediately after climbing up, we came across a long corridor with a row of chairs arranged horizontally against the walls. At the end was a desk where a lady was sitting, typing something frivolously on her desktop. Her typing just felt off and didn't make sense. She kept pushing the 'ctrl' button for no reason. Something felt off about the clinic, too. There were no patients here.

"Um…excuse me, mam," Rohit asked the lady, "could you tell us whether there is a girl called Akriti here? She is the daughter of the owner of this clinic."

"Are you her friends?"

"Yes," I said.

"Please sit, I'll let her know you are here," said the lady as she left through a door next to the desk.

Our faces filled with joy. We had finally found her. But why had she been ignoring us? Was she ok? Why didn't she come to school?

A few minutes had passed when the door opened. Rohit and I got up to greet Akriti.

Only it wasn't Akriti who came through the door. Two tall and bulky-looking men wearing black suits came through the door and approached us.

They stared at us, and we stared at them.

Then one of them finally spoke. "Which one of you is Anirudh?"

How do they know my name? I was confused. My heart buzzed as it sensed danger. I wanted to speak, but I was too scared.

"Where is Akriti?" Rohit asked, "And who are you?"

"Look kid," the man said, placing his hand on Rohit's shoulder, "Just answer my question."

I could feel the strength with which the man was pressing Rohit's shoulder. And I could feel the fear in Rohit's body. I was about to intervene and identify myself but…

Bang!

The man holding Rohit immediately fell to the ground. The other man turned to face the attacker but was kicked hard in his groin and immediately fell to the ground.

And there stood Akriti, holding a fire extinguisher in her hand.

"We need to go now," she said in a rather raspy voice as she tried to catch her breath.

"Go where?" I asked.

She then grabbed our hands and started pulling us down the stairs. Leaving the fire extinguisher on the ground.

"There's no time to explain," she said.

She then left hold of our hands and then started running down the stairs.

"Just run after me!" she screamed.

Rohit and I looked at each other, nodded in unison, and ran after her.

She took us around the building and then towards a red-coloured Hyundai i10 parked under a tree.

But then she surprised us by opening the car door with keys she took out of her pocket, sitting inside the car, and starting it, while we stood at the back of the car staring in confusion.

"Get in the car! What are you waiting for?" She shouted after popping her head out the window.

We got in the back seat, still dazed by what Akriti was thinking. The car moved forward and out of the building compound.

Akriti was actually driving the car!

One of the men whom Akriti had brought down was now just next to the gate and tried to stop the car, but Akriti drove off anyway. Almost running him over.

"What is going on, Akriti?" Rohit asked.

"Yeah, and how the heck are you driving a car?" I asked.

"By using my hands and my feet."

"Seriously Akriti?" Rohit said.

"Look, there is no time to explain. Let us first get out of here. They will be after us."

"Who?" I asked.

"Just shut up! And let me drive for a second!"

Akriti sped along the road like a maniac.

Did she really know how to drive? Why was she not picking up our calls? How did that bulky man know my name? What is going on?

"Alright, we are approaching a checkpoint. Just don't say anything," Akriti said.

I had noticed that checkpoint quite a few times before and wondered why there was a checkpoint in our neighbourhood. Was it because of us? Had the government figured out that I was the reverter?

Akriti was driving normally now, the checkpoint visible 500 meters ahead.

Soon, the car came to a stop. There were a few cars ahead of us and the police checked each of them. After a minute, it was our turn.

The windows slid down and two scrawny policemen peered inside. After looking at the interior, one of them near the driver's window asked Akriti, "License, madam."

Akriti opened the glove box and took out a card. The policeman looked at it for 2 seconds and then gave her the signal that she was allowed to leave. The glove box was closed, and we moved forward.

After the checkpoint was long gone (about 5 minutes). Akriti turned right into the pay and park of a small multiplex.

"Why are we going to the multiplex?" I asked.

"And will you explain everything to us now?" Rohit asked.

"No, we are just here to change cars so that it would be harder for them to track us. There are no cameras in and around this pay and park."

"So you won't explain a thing?" Rohit asked.

"We're worried, Akriti," I said.

"I know Anirudh. The only reason I am not saying anything is because it would be too stressful for me. And I am under a lot of stress already."

Akriti parked the car and said, "Quick! Follow me!" She shut the engine and got out of the car.

We ran behind her to another car, which was a white Ertiga.

We drove for another hour along the Western Express highway. Soon Akriti turned into Aarey colony. A forested area within the eco-sensitive zone of the Sanjay Gandhi National Park. I only ever went through it to reach Navi Mumbai, but where was Akriti taking us?

Trees green frivolled past us as we sped along the soft black asphalt. After half an hour Akriti stopped the car at the entrance of a villa.

"We've reached. It will take a lot of time for them to track us now. We should be safe for some time," she said.

There was an awfully quiet atmosphere here, except for the birds. High rises of Goregaon were visible in the distance and a vast lush foliage before it. All this greenery issued a sense of calm over my body.

The villa itself was a white, two-storey building, of not too special architecture. It was surrounded by a circle of green grass. Water drained from the balconies as if it had just rained, but it was more of an indication of the rooms having been recently cleaned.

The villa, however, made me feel uncomfortable for some reason.

"You know you can't stay here for long, right?" a middle-aged man asked Akriti as we entered the uncanny abode.

"Yes, just for the night."

Then the man looked at me for a few seconds and asked Akriti, "That's him, right?"

To which Akriti nodded.

"I can't believe it!"

"None of us did at first, but he really is a time traveller."

"Us?"

"Rohit and I."

"Who's Rohit?" Then Rohit took a step forward and spoke. "I am Rohit. Anirudh's best friend. Now If you two are done...and I mean no disrespect...but can someone explain what the heck is going on?!"

"Akriti, the sofa is right next to you, and I'll...I'll go bring some snacks," the man said as he swiftly turned around and started walking away.

"Wait! Don't let me do this alone!"

"They're your friends!"

And he was out of sight.

Akriti then smiled her ridiculously heartwarming smile (God, I missed that smile) and directed us towards the sofa.

"Please sit guys."

And we sat down.

Akriti looked at the ground and then back at us a few times until Rohit also put on a ridiculous but not heartwarming smile and said, "Dear Akriti, will you say something?"

Akriti's smile disappeared. She sighed and said, "I...I work for R&AW as a trainee agent and they think that 'The Reverter' is a terrorist organisation and I am a part of it as well."

What was I?

Stunned.

No.

Stunned *and* petrified.

"I don't believe this Akriti," I said.

"Oh, but I know you do, Anirudh," she said, smiling.

And I did. It did explain her behaviour these past three months.

Not that it wasn't absolutely crazy!

The Truth

XIV

My hands were trembling as I thought of the implications of what Akriti said. If R&AW knew who I was, I couldn't imagine what would happen to me once they caught me, and what would they do to our parents? Especially if they thought I was operating some terrorist organisation!

But more questions needed answers.

"Wait, wait, wait," Rohit blurted, "Since when are you in R&AW?"

"I was recruited four years ago."

"When you were 11 years old?" I asked.

Akriti smiled, looked at the ground, and slowly looked at us again. Then she turned her gaze to the left and back. She stared at us again for a few seconds and finally opened her mouth to say something…but closed it again.

"What is it, Akriti?" Rohit said, annoyed.

"Whatever you have to say, just say it," I said.

Akriti clenched her fists and looked down, "I am actually 23 years old right now…that's why I have a driver's licence."

"So everything you have told us about yourself is a complete lie? Your name's not even Akriti right?" Rohit said.

"No, most of it is true…the only thing that isn't true besides what I have already told you is that I don't work as a nurse at the hospital because I want to become a doctor, it's because I was assigned to go undercover and provide monthly observation reports as part of training."

"At a hospital? How would that work? What would you report on?... It's a hospital," I asked.
"They would sometimes send suspicious people without me knowing, and I would need to identify them as potential threats. I thought you, Anirudh, were one of those people. And since you were in my class, I thought maybe you could potentially be a trainee agent as well and were potentially trying to investigate me or were sent by R&AW."
"Wow!" Rohit started laughing.
"That turned out pretty well, right?" I said, trying to control my laughter. Akriti started laughing as well.
"But does your grandfather actually own the hospital?" Rohit asked.
"Yeah, that is true, but he isn't a part of R&AW nor does he know about our involvement with R&AW."

The middle-aged man entered the room with a tray full of snacks in his hand.
"Well, it seems you are getting along," he said.
"Oh yeah, I am happy that we at least found Akriti. But I need more answers," Rohit said.
"And sorry, if this sounds rude, but who are you?" I asked.
"Oh no! I am sorry I didn't introduce myself! I thought Akriti told you about me!" he said, keeping the tray on the coffee table.
"No, she has a habit of hiding things," Rohit said.
"Not fair dude!" Akriti screeched.
"Oh, it's fair enough," I said with a giggle.

Akriti stared at me in disbelief. I stared back smiling.
"My name is Gulpreet Singh and I work under Akriti's father."

"Wait, you said your father was a doctor," I said.

Akriti smiled and then covered her face with her hands in embarrassment.

"Her father is the chief of domestic operations for R&AW. That clinic you just ran from is actually a front for local operations and communication," Mr Gulpreet said.

"Damn Akriti!" Rohit said.

"But when we were at the clinic, there were no patients. Usually, there would be a lot of patients at a clinic in an area like that…I mean, even if it is just a front." I asked him.

"Yeah, that's because of Akriti."

"Care to explain why Akriti? And what about your indifference towards us for these past months? You know how haphazard our channel has been without you?" Rohit said to Akriti.

Since we couldn't communicate properly, we missed dates of important events and we had to end up releasing that 'major reveal' video because it would be too late if we didn't, but it led to people not believing in us anymore. I knew it would turn out like that, but Rohit insisted on doing it.

Akriti lifted her face and said, "Yes. I'll continue from the part where I thought Anirudh was there to investigate me."

"Sure," I said.

"Remember when I said the walls are paper thin? At the hospital? They weren't. I was trying to eavesdrop on you two. And when you two started talking about time travelling, I felt that you knew I was there. Now I knew that I had to confront you directly, to challenge you to reveal yourself. But you didn't yield and continued rambling about the future, which I do believe is true now…or maybe that was what you wanted me to believe (if you were from R&AW that is). And on the day you gave us a bunch of predictions about what would happen in the class, I concluded that the entire class and some teachers were somehow involved in my test. But that was also when I started doubting my theory about you being someone from R&AW. But the alternative was that you were an actual time traveller. which...really appeared ridiculous at that time...but then I started pushing for you to 'warn the world' to get something out of you again, for you to fumble and break cover, or just give me some indication that you are not a time traveller and have been sent by R&AW, which you did, but not in the way I thought. But then Rohit did something that did not make sense, because if Rohit was involved with R&AW according to my theory, then he wouldn't have been motivating you to make the video as well. Your reason for not wanting to tell the world also didn't make a lot of sense, which made me continue with my theory of you being connected with R&AW but there was no certainty. But then, right before the earthquake happened, all of my theories about your connection with R&AW were shattered. R&AW contacted me to give me the order to look into 'The Reverter' as they are a terrorist organisation that is possibly operating from the neighbourhood I am in. And I knew that they were absolutely serious about this and were not testing me because it was a direct order from my father. And then the earthquake happened...which complicated things even further as I had realised that you really were a time traveller and R&AW was telling me that the earthquake was possibly caused by the Reverter."

Then Akriti became silent. She started staring at the ground. But after two seconds, she spoke.

"Another problem was that you two were my first proper friends in a long time and I had come to love you guys. No matter the age gap, I really wanted to be proper friends with you. And now there was a deep guilt inside that made me go into depression for the first time since my mother's death."

A teardrop slipped past Akriti's cheek.

"I felt that I had betrayed the only friends I ever had. And then I couldn't see eye to eye with you guys…I really did consider you two good friends. Because I knew if my theory of you two being from R&AW was true, we all could still be friends and I liked you two a lot. And then R&AW had been pressuring me to give them some intel…I didn't know what to do."

More tears slipped. Each of them felt like a waterfall.

"All you needed to do was tell us," Rohit said.

"I agree, Akriti. We were your friends, and we cared about you. We still do!" I said.

"I know," Akriti said, her lips turning into another heartwarming smile. We smiled back.

"I mean, you guys actually came to the clinic to search for me."

"We did," Rohit said.

"I am sorry," She said.

"It's fine now"

I was feeling pretty good now. We stared at each other smiling for a few seconds. And then I spoke, realising what was at stake, "Alright, R&AW is after us, please continue Akriti."

"Yeah, so…I finally decided that I was going to go tell them the absolute truth, no matter how ridiculous it would have sounded. Weirdly that day, you two also came to search for me. They didn't believe me, of course, but they did tell me a few things."

"What?" Rohit asked.

"The most important thing they told me was that the investigation began because of a series of patterned EMFs noticed across the globe each time our videos were uploaded and on some other days, which I realised included the days on which Anirudh had fainted and the day of the earthquake."

"That's interesting," Rohit said.

"Yeah, they think that the EMFs are a form of communication for our 'terrorist' organization."

That was very interesting indeed. I needed to dig more into this. Hell, I needed to research everything that had happened to me. I had spent enough time not thinking about how I came here. And apparently, I am the only one who can save this world from 'him'. I have been doing nothing about it for a long time. It was time to make a move.

"Also, where were all the patients again?" Rohit asked.

"Since they knew that I was coming to give them intel, they cancelled all appointments that day and told everyone who came otherwise that the doctors had gone for a conference. What they didn't expect were you two. The 'receptionist' told me about it and I ran out of there. And you know the rest. They were already convinced that I had joined the organisation, and was trying to cover for them by talking nonsense about time travel."

"But do they know who we are?" I asked.

"Yes," Akriti replied, "they are not sure as to how we are involved in this but they know we 'know' something but they…"

She was interrupted by Rohit, "And what about our parents and our family?"

At that moment the room was so quiet, that you could hear the tiniest insect walking on the wall.

But then Akriti said it…

"They will be interrogated."

There are no words that could describe the dread I felt at that moment.

"What do you mean, interrogated?" Rohit said, his voice trembling.

Akriti remained silent, but Mr Gulpreet spoke, "They will be questioned about everything and anything they could know about you. Don't worry, they won't be tortured or anything. At

Least Akriti's dad won't let that happen. But I am not sure about Mr Chandra from the N.I.A. He is currently heading the investigation. But again, Akriti's father won't let that happen. He knows that her dear Akriti and her friends can't be terrorists."

This is the reason I wanted to refrain from doing anything about anything. I knew I should have just gone with living my life normally. I should have never told them anything about the future. I should have just lived my second chance quietly and happily until it all ended. I should have stopped when that entity told me to stop.

I looked at Rohit and Akriti. Their eyes bulged with fear. Akriti seemed like she was about to cry.

"I could have told you all sooner. Why was I so stupid?" She said.

"What can we do now, Akriti?" I asked.

"I don't know, But we can't stay here for long. We must leave as soon as possible,"

"And go where Akriti?" Rohit asked, "RA&W will have the whole city sealed by tomorrow."

"I'll think of something. Just rest for now," Akriti said as she got up and headed into the bathroom.

The room remained quiet for a long time. Akriti had come out of the bathroom but went into another room. She was blaming herself for it. I wished there was something I could do. Something that would end all of this.

Only you can save the world now

The words of the entity echoed in my head as I sat and stared at the white tiles of the floor.

"But how? The only thing I have done is travel back in time," I said out loud.

"What?" Rohit asked.

"Oh…I guess I said that out loud. Remember what that entity told me during the earthquake?"
"Yes," Rohit said.
"Akriti told me about these visions you have been having," Mr Gulpreeet said, "it was something along the lines of 'only you can save the world' right?"
"Yes!" I said.
"And then you just spoke about how you can save the world," Mr Gulpreet said.
"Yes, the only thing I have done is travel back in time. And my thinking ability has increased, but that is it."
"Do you have any idea about how you travelled back in time?" Mr Gulpreet questioned.
And then it hit me.
"Yeah, how did I travel back in time? More specifically, why did only my consciousness travel back in time? The answer to how I could save the world must lie within the answer to this question!"

Rohit and Mr Gulpreet smiled.

"It might be," Rohit said.
"I remember the other-worldly experience I had felt when I had supposedly died. The tranquillity, the feeling of nothingness, the weightlessness, the non-ability to feel my body."
"You need to tell us more about it, Anirudh," Mr Gulpreet said.
"After the blast occurred, everything went dark, but I was not feeling anything, not my weight or my body, only my mind. Imagine if someone blindfolded you, took out your ears and dropped you from a great height inside a vacuum chamber. I mean it is hard to imagine, but that is what I felt…yet there was more. Something that felt like it reassuring me that everything was alright…and then I find myself in my 2019 room,"

"But your body was that of a 15-year-old and it was only your consciousness that had travelled, right?" Mr Gulpreet.

"Then is there something that you know but you don't know that you know?" Rohit said

"Yes, could this be it? Could my consciousness be the weapon I need to save the world?"

"Only you can tell us that, Anirudh," Mr Gulpreet said.

"I remember my 12th standard class on quantum physics and the countless YouTube videos I had seen on subatomic particles. The hadrons, the quarks, the mesons and the bosons and the phenomenon of quantum entanglement and so on….my mind is fixating on that for some reason."

"Quantum what?" Rohit asked, to which Mr Gulpreet replied, "Quantum entanglement. In quantum entanglement, two particles have their properties connected in such a way that if you did something to one, the other would show something as well, no matter how far apart you would keep them. The particles could be kept on the poles of the earth, one on Earth and the other on Pluto, or even keep them across the entire universe and maybe even across time!"

"Yes! Was that how my consciousness was able to travel back? With some form of entanglement between a group of particles of the past?"

"But quantum entanglement certainly doesn't work like that. At least that wasn't how it was theorised to be, or maybe…I would have to do some calculations, and maybe even experiments, to which I no longer have access." Mr Gulpreet said.

"How do you know so much about it, Mr Gulpreet?" Rohit asked.

"Yeah, I am surprised that you know about it," I said.

"Yes, I was a physics professor at IIT Kharagpur before I was recruited by RA&W. I have a PhD in physics."

"That is fantastic!" I said.
"Wow, sir! Can you please write a letter of recommendation for me, sir?" Rohit said, laughing. We all laughed as well.
"Another theory comes to my mind: Time crystals," I said.

Along with time crystals, I also came to hypothesise a very fascinating thing.
"That sounds fancy…what are they?" Rohit asked.
"These are structures that have been suggested as a possible way to manipulate time and space. They are based on the idea that certain particles can be arranged in a specific pattern that creates a periodic time-like symmetry, allowing them to move in time without being affected by it…I mean sort of...They were_first detected in 2016 in experiments with ions of the rare-earth metal ytterbium at the University of Maryland. In 2021, a team at Google developed the world's first 'time crystal' in one of their quantum computers," I said.

Then Mr Gulpreet spoke, "They will develop a time crystal in 2021? I have read the theory and about the experiments at Aalto University, but they shouldn't be possible as the time crystals resemble a perpetual motion machine. The total working energy of a system can only decrease. It should be impossible for them just to exist or to create them for sustained periods."
"They said that the quantum changes in low-energy states of the nuclei in time crystals neither create nor use energy, so the total energy of such a system never increases."
Mr Gulpreet went into deep thought. After a while, he said, "OK, but what does that have to do with your time travelling?"
"What if the entire universe, along with every particle, was a time crystal?"

The eyes of both Mr. Gulpreet and Rohit, who had been listening intently, widened in unison.

"And you Anirudh, somehow found a way to break out of its perpetual time cycle....I mean, it honestly doesn't make too much sense, but then there is so little that we know about the quantum phenomenon. What you are saying could have happened. We need to think more. We might actually be on to something."

"Yes, but we need to discuss more and research it. Maybe the nuclear blast was responsible for it? Remember what that dark entity said? 'You shouldn't be here. How are you here?' "

"Wait, could it be that you actually met God?" Rohit asked.

"That thing in my first dreams couldn't be a God."

"Then you met the Devil," said Mr Gulpreet.

"But then the other one who warned you could be God!" Rohit said.

"Maybe, and at this point, I can't say anything about that, but it is possible," I said.

"But we must get moving Anirudh, we need to discuss and research before you go from here. And if that God is dying...then we have no time before the Devil, or whatever takes over. I mean, you are literally seeing a red sky, right?" Mr Gulpreet said.

"Yes, but the sky is now black."

Mr Gulpreet seemed to be shocked on hearing that.

"Alright then come with me you two to my study room," he said. And with that, we began looking into everything.

After hours of discussion and calculation on a whiteboard (Rohit had slept in his chair and Akriti was silently reading a book in the corner of the room) we had come to some fascinating conclusions.

Section 212

XV

The study room was a mini library with wooden bookshelves on all sides. A large oval table in the middle of the room had some books on it (that Mr Gulpreet and I had gone through several times). There were 4 chairs in total in the room, one occupied by Akriti—as I told you earlier—reading some classic novel. The other was occupied by Rohit, blissfully sleeping with his mouth wide open–we tried to close it several times–in front of a whiteboard with lots of calculations. And the remaining chairs were inhabited by Mr Gulpreet and me.

It was almost 10 pm now, and we had come to some fascinating conclusions.

"Are you guys done?" Akriti asked, popping her head out of the book.

"Yes," I said.

Akriti stood up and kept her book on the oval table.

"Then tell me about what you have been discussing for so long."

I hadn't noticed Akriti being in the room until I noticed Rohit sleeping. Which was about 2 hours into our discussion. She must have been waiting for a long time now.

Our school ends at 3:00 pm and I usually reach home by 4:00 pm but we got down to go to the clinic at around 3:35 pm, and it then took us about 5 minutes to reach the clinic from where it took us about 45 minutes to Mr Gulpreet's house, which means

we started our discussion at about 5:30 pm (adding 10 minutes for our conversation with Akriti about her truth). So we had been discussing it for approximately 4 and a half hours!
"We should probably wake up Rohit," Mr Gulpreet said.

Akriti went and shook Rohit, who jolted awake, snorting his drool up and then going into a coughing fit. He was fine after a few seconds.
"Sorry, I fell asleep. Did you guys figure it out?" Rohit said, "Oh, hi Akriti!"
"Good morning sleepy pants," Akriti said.
"Or should you say good night? It's 10 now," I said.
"Wait What? It's 10 already? You should have woken me up sooner!"
"Yes, he's right, and aren't you all hungry?" Akriti said.
"Oh yeah, I'll quickly make something and we will discuss our findings over dinner. What do you say?" Mr Gulpreet asked.

We all nodded.

There wasn't much time, so Mr Gulpreet quickly made some of the tastiest chilli paneer and parathas I had ever eaten. It was made within half an hour, with Akriti helping him as well, while I explained quantum mechanics to Rohit. He surprisingly understood things pretty well!
"My brain works very fast when I have just woken up," he said.

After a while of eating, Akriti asked Mr Gulpreet to begin explaining our conclusions.
"So here it is," said Mr Gulpreet, "As Anirudh said, What if the entire universe was a time crystal? What if the entire universe together periodically switched between low-energy and high-energy states? Like a bunch of whack-a-moles popping up and down, they seem to be randomly doing so, but we know that there is a pattern which repeats. What if the whole universe worked exactly like that?

Like a computer program, what if it repeated its patterned high and low energy state shifts for each subatomic particle in the entire universe? Now we humans don't completely understand the phenomenon of time crystals. And 'Time Crystals' is just a cool name given to something that has nothing to do with actual time travel, but considering that if the entire universe entered a time crystal-like state for a few cycles, it's fascinating how at the subatomic level it could mean that the whole universe went back in time like Anirudh, periodically."

Akriti and Rohit nodded in thought, munching on the paratha-paneer mixture.

"Also, here is what we can comment on the weird beings that I have dreamed of," I said. "So far, we know that there are two beings: One is evil and One is good. The good one was possibly in control of our universe and the evil one wanted control...which it might have completely gotten by now."

"But we don't see much change, do we," Mr Gulpreet said, "except, of course, Anirudh, to whom the sky appears black. And there arises a question."

"Why do only I see so many changes? Why did I travel back in time when I should have died?"

"And the Answer might lie in our theory of time crystals. What if the universe was at a reset point when the nuclear blast happened? The nuclear blast which was supposed to kill Anirudh? So possibly the universe reset and we went back to the day Anirudh says to have come back. Only Anirudh, for some reason, wasn't reset completely. But why? Why only Anirudh?"

"One argument against time crystals was that they operated like a perpetual motion machine. And like all perpetual motion machines, it wouldn't sustain itself. It would need some form of external energy to replenish the cycle."

"And we think that the beings we talked about provide that energy, and hence control the world."

Rohit's and Akriti's eyes widened on realising this. They continued to eat.

"Yes! And the evil being that I saw in my first and second dreams, was surprised to see me there…wherever *there* is…it's a question in itself…but I vividly remember it saying, *How are you here? You shouldn't be here."*

"Then the evil being tried to stop Anirudh from announcing himself to the world, by scaring him and threatening to explode the world. But Anirudh didn't stop. He announced his existence to the world and that brought the attention of the good being towards Anirudh. It told him that only he could save the world. There must be something special about Anirudh, and Anirudh must soon figure it out…but we do think it is related to the time crystals and Anirudh's consciousness."

Akriti had stopped eating, and so did Rohit. Both of them were now staring at us.

"So what do we do? How can Anirudh figure this out? I do think we are running out of time," Rohit said.

"I don't know, but I think I am getting close to figuring it out," I said as I took a piece of the paratha in my mouth. But the truth was that I knew nothing about what I could do to stop the world from the clutches of the evil being.

"That's it?" Akriti asked.

"Yes," said Mr Gulpreet.

"But that only states an incomplete explanation of things that are happening, which is just a guess at best," Akriti complained.

Mr Gulpreet sighed as he tore a piece of the paratha.

"Yes Akriti, but it is the best thing we could come up with," he said.

"How are you going to figure it out? How the heck are you supposed to save the world?" asked Rohit.
"I think there is an answer out there and I will find it. If a godly being can trust me, why can't you?" I said.
"The Godly being had no choice!" Akriti said.

The room was silent. All that could be heard was the clanking of chilli paneer bowls with the plates for a while as everyone resumed eating.
"So, have you planned anything, Akriti?" Mr Gulpreet asked, breaking the silence.
"Yes," she said.

And the room was silent again but, I broke the silence.
"Where are we going? Will we be safe there?"
"It's the last place they would look. And I wouldn't tell you in front of Mr Gulpreet."
"But why?" Rohit asked.
"The less I know, the better it will be for everyone."

I understood what he meant.
"You will be interrogated as well," I said.

Neither Akriti nor Mr Gulpreet said anything. Rohit just stared at me.

This was not fair at all. I needed to figure out what I needed to do, and I needed to figure it out fast. We did not have time. We never did.

But at least we had a little more clarity now. Somehow, the entire universe had shifted back to a different time, and my consciousness didn't. My consciousness was probably the single most powerful thing in this universe at this moment. And I was ready to do whatever it would take to save this world.

After dinner, we all went to sleep. Mr Gulpreet had given us some clothes to wear and we finally got out of our school uniform (We should have changed our clothes long ago). Rohit and I slept on two separate mattresses in the living room, while Akriti had a separate bed in another room. Mr Gulpreet slept in his room, which made me wonder: Why was Mr Gulpreet living alone in a place like this?

But I already had a lot of questions that needed pondering, so I decided to forget about it and go to sleep.

And this time I had a dream.

It was obviously not a normal dream.

I was lying…no, floating on something. I tried to upright myself and realised that I was neck deep in water with no surface that my feet could touch. I waddled my arms around to stay afloat. There was water all around me, and it was crimson red. A very deep and agonising red colour. The ocean stretched to the horizon all around me. But the sky was white. Completely white.

I was staring at the blank sky for a very long time now. The calmness it gave me, couldn't be expressed in words. Just pure bliss. Exactly how I had felt after the blast that sent me to 2019.

But soon the sky's brightness dimmed, and it became black, except for a small circle of light on the horizon. Which felt like the sun was rising. But it was not rising at all.

The peering white light seemed to cry, but I didn't know why. Even the water appeared black except that I could hear it screaming. Screaming at me to go away, to go away and die.

I started swimming towards the light. The circle of light slowly started becoming bigger, just like the cave in my dream at Akriti's house.

But suddenly, the light began expanding rapidly and covered the entire sky. But it didn't stop. It started growing downwards.

Like a white wall, I could feel it coming down and getting blindingly bright. The red colour of the water was turning snow white.

Soon it had reached my head and started pushing me down. I tried to resist it, but all the struggle only resulted in me going further down the water. And soon, I was completely submerged.

But being under the water didn't feel like being underwater. Firstly, I could breathe. Secondly, I was not in the water at all! I was gliding in the sky with a heavily forested area visible beneath me. A few hill structures protruded outwards: brown nuggets in the middle of lush green foliage.

And I said that I was gliding, not falling. It was a rather slow descent, like an angel coming from heaven. And soon I had landed on top of a hill. It was a small hill with one or two trees and no grass. The air was fresh and cold. The atmosphere was completely opposite of the hell I had fallen from.

But the hill felt oddly familiar. I felt like I had been here before.

I looked around, and I could see some buildings on the horizon. And that's when I realized I was on top of the Kanheri Caves in Sanjay Gandhi National Park!

Then I heard the giggling of a small girl. I began moving towards the sound. Then, I discovered some stairs going down the hill. I could see a large ground the size of a swimming pool surrounded by trees on all sides, except the one facing the hill. And in the middle was a small girl playing with…Mr Gulpreet?

I reached down and started going towards the girl and Mr Gulpreet.

"Hello!" I shouted. They stopped playing and looked at me.

The girl had a very confused look on her face. She looked like she had seen a ghost.

"Anirudh?" The little girl said, still dazed from seeing me.

BANG!

I heard a loud bang. Like a bomb had just exploded somewhere and everything suddenly turned black. I was feeling weightless. I was floating in…What? I didn't know…And then I woke up.

"Good! You woke up! We are leaving," Akriti said as she was standing with Rohit, packing a bag.

"Don't shout Akriti, you will wake Mr Gulpreet," Rohit said.

The dream didn't make any sense. What happened there? Why was Mr Gulpreet in it?

What was that Red Sea? The light? Who was the girl? What was that bang?

"Did you have a dream, Anirudh?" Akriti asked. Rohit stopped packing and stared at me. Akriti had probably noticed me in distress.

"What happened?" He asked.

Then I proceeded to explain the dream.

"Wait…I had the same dream! I mean the part where you saw a little girl. In my dream, I was playing with Mr Gulpreet and then I saw you! And then the dream ended," Akriti said.

"What?" I said.

"How is that possible?" Rohit asked.

"Why would I lie about this?" Akriti said.

"...but…" I was immediately interrupted by Akriti, "Oh! And I had this dream yesterday!"

"That doesn't really help Akriti," I said.

"Maybe it does! That is how I got the idea of coming here to Mr Gulpreet's house if something bad happened when I had gone to confess at the clinic. And that is also how I got the idea of going to the Kanheri Caves!"

"You are going to the Kanheri Caves? Very smart!" said Mr Gulpreet as he entered the living room.

"Yes," Akriti said with her face sullen.
"Well, go on then!"
"But what about you, sir?" Rohit asked.
"Don't worry about me. I am a R&AW agent, after all!"
"Thank you for all you have done for us," I said.

Then Akriti went and hugged Mr Gulpreet.

He hugged her back.

"It will all be ok," he said, wiping a tear off of Akriti's face.
"May you save the world!" He said to all of us.

I smiled and said, "We will, and I think my dream has told me that the Kanheri Caves is exactly the place we need to go."

Or maybe it was a place I shouldn't go to. I didn't know.

The sound of the car's engine seemed to do a good job of muffling Akriti's sobs.

***

"Where have they gone?!" Chandra shouted at Mr Gulpreet. Small drops of his saliva were visible.

"Akriti is a very smart girl, Chandra. They packed up in the middle of the night and left."

The team from R&AW and NIA arrived at Mr Gulpreet's house at 10:00 am.

Rather, I should say, '*he*' arrived at 10:00 am.

"You do know that harbouring criminals is a punishable offence?" Chandra said.

"But I didn't know she had committed a crime! Also, what crime has she committed?"

"Do not act so Aloof!"

"That's enough Chandra!" said Mr Prakash.

"Ok, the father of the terrorist has spoken. Besides, I already know where to go. Officers! apprehend Mr Gulpreet and send him to headquarters for further questioning." Chandra said as he turned back and headed outside.

Mr Prakash and Mr Gulpreet shared a look of concern before the other officers put cuffs on Mr Gulpreet's hands and took him away.

"We don't have all day Prakash sir!" Chandra shouted from inside the car.

The clock was ticking. And it was ticking fast.

All is calm. All is right. All is well.

XVI

"Why did we ditch the car again?" Rohit complained.
"So that it is harder to track us. Don't you have something better to talk about than just whining? Crack a joke or something!" Akriti said as she turned back to answer. The heat of the damp forest must have been getting to her.

Why are we in a forest all of a sudden, you ask?

After we left Mr Gulpreet's house, we drove for some time along the road until we came across an outpost visible in the distance. A tall tower protruded upwards in the middle of the dense foliage. Akriti told us to get out of the car and left us standing there for a few minutes. Meanwhile, she took the car back in the direction we came from and parked it at the side of the road. There was a small wildlife viewing spot nearby, so some other cars were parked around and facing the same direction as our car.

"To blend the car in," she said as she came back from the parked vehicle. But why didn't we 'blend' the car in the parking area of the Kanheri Caves? Why blend it 8 km away from it?

There is only one way to get to Kanheri Caves by car and it is infested with police outposts. If we were to go there normally, it would have been impossible to avoid them. Even if they weren't specifically looking for us, their surveillance cameras would capture us. So we had to take a 'shortcut'. A very long 'shortcut', through the forest.

Therefore, we started walking through the forest. No police to worry about, only mosquitoes filled with malaria and dengue viruses and leopards drooling at the sight of fresh teenage meat roaming around.

I had to ask her, "Akriti, are you sure this is safe?"

"You too?!" Akriti whined.

"Who's whining now?" Rohit snickered.

"Why are you so annoying, Rohit?" Akriti asked. Her face was flustered.

"Nevermind him Akriti. You tell me if this is safe. Because I highly doubt it is," I said.

Despite my fears, I wasn't sensing any presence of a predator. The birds were chirping as usual. Monkeys could be seen peacefully eating fruits (except for some of them, who were having a gang war). The jungle was quite noisy. Which indicated the absence of a predator. But for how long would this peace last? How long before a leopard jumps onto us from these dark trees?

"Ok, yes, walking through a forest is dangerous…but it will be fine…trust me, I…I have done this before."

"When you were five years old with Mr Gulpreet?" I said.

Akriti didn't reply to that and just looked forward. But after a moment of silence, she finally said, "How is it that you were in my dream? How did we share the same…no, similar dream? That too, a day apart?"

"Yeah, it doesn't make any sense!" Rohit said.

"I have been thinking about it…I think that the good being saved me from the bad one by bringing me into your dream. And I am starting to believe that my dreams are some sort of connection to their 'world' and their 'world' is somehow connected to everyone's consciousness. The place has to do something with me being the only one who can save the world. Maybe the being specifically sent me in that dream and maybe it wanted us to go to Kanheri Caves. I think there could be some answers we can find there…it's a lot…but it feels like a puzzle coming together."

"That is interesting…but it is still just a speculation, Anirudh," she said.

"Even if it is just a speculation, it is definitely something to think about and could very well be true," Rohit said.

"Which could very well be just ramblings of a madman!" Akriti screamed. Her face was angrier now.

We all stopped. I stared at Akriti. She stared back but quickly calmed herself.

But she wasn't wrong, was she? It had occurred to me before that maybe I was suffering from some kind of schizophrenia or something. I was putting everyone in danger. Maybe the evil entity taking over was my fault as well.

"I'm sorry, I didn't mean to…"

"I understand," I said.

"It's just that…"

"Your brain blames me for everything that has gone wrong with your life. You have been branded as a terrorist and have been forced to travel through this humid jungle with kids…I mean a kid and a 21-year-old in a 15-year-old body,"

"I don't blame you! No! It's not your fault!"

"I am not a kid!" Rohit butted in. Ignoring him, I continued,

"But it is! I could have just not done anything and lived my life like a normal person enjoying a second chance at life, but here I am! Me trying to change the course of the future has probably doomed this world! It's all my fault! You all should go back…I will just figure it out on my own. Tell them that I blackmailed you or something. Just…leave me! I am a madman, after all, right?"

"No, Anirudh!" Akriti was about to start crying.

Or maybe the heat was getting me too.

We all were just standing there. Rohit tried to say something but refrained.

Everything felt dismal. What was I doing here? Why did I travel to 2019? Was it all just an illusion? Had I never even been a time traveller? Did my brain just make stuff up?

But then I realized…thinking about this was pointless. Wasn't it me who made all the correct predictions? Wasn't it these two convinced me to go ahead with telling the whole world about my predictions? Why was I at fault?

Time was ticking, and we needed to go.

"Let's go," I said, "we should reach there before it gets closed."

Akriti wiped her face, turned back, and continued walking forward. I followed. Rohit stood there silently for a while, but eventually came after us.

We walked silently. I couldn't think of anything for most of the walk. I was just lost in the pathetic bitterness of the world.

But then I looked at the sky above. If not for the watch I was wearing, I would never be able to tell the time. The black sky was unwaveringly still. There were no clouds. The bitterness had now turned to a certain mix of fear and intrigue. Just a completely black sky. Why?

The dream I had yesterday had clouds. The sky was not black at all! Was that an indication of something?

The white light that pushed me into Akriti's dream…that place…I think the place where the dream takes place is real. All our dreams exist somewhere. The dreams in which I came in contact with the beings exist somewhere. And all dreams are connected. They must be! It's not a puzzle coming together! That place is the answer! But so far, I have only been able to access it through my dreams. Or maybe it's not the dreams that exist somewhere, but our consciousness is connected. Maybe humanity is a hive mind?

Interesting thought…but failingly pointless.

We walked for a long while. With a half an hour break in between. After a total of 3 hours of walking, we reached the Kanheri Caves or at least the back of it.

A vast open pasture was visible with a large rocky wall in front of us. A cool breeze blew at our faces, which felt like a heavy burden had been lifted. It was the same place we saw in Akriti's and mine shared dream. This was the same place where Akriti played with Mr Gulpreet. The same place where I had been thrown down.

"This place does bring back memories," Akriti said.

"Akriti, can you tell us about this and why I saw you play with Mr Gulpreet?" I asked.

"After my mother's accident Mr Gulpreet asked us to come to stay with him for some time," she said, "this place was and is closed off to the public, but Mr Gulpreet knew how to get here through the forest as we did. We used to come here every Sunday. It used to be his weekly trek before I came, anyway. It was a lot of fun for me and took my mind off the tragedy."

Akriti stared at the field longingly, as if searching for something. Her eyes glistened like diamonds in the dark.

The Sun shone on the rocky hill in front of us. Colouring it a golden yellow. The black sky above it made it seem like Mount Olympus—with the Greek Gods waiting at the top to watch the end of the world.

"I am sorry, Anirudh," she said as she looked back at me.

"It's alright," I said. "You do understand that we are all in this together?"

"Of course we are," she said.

"Then let's not fight each other. This is none of our faults," I said.
"I..." Rohit said, "Wanna say something..."

We looked at him curiously.

"I am tired...of everything. And I know you are too. I don't know what is happening out there in the world, what is happening to our parents—it has only been one day, but every aspect of our life has changed," Rohit said.

That one word, 'parents', sent my heart throbbing.

"But I do know that we will prevail. Whatever darkness is upon us will meet its end, and together, we will save our world."

"You are right," Akriti said, "we will prevail!"

"Yep!" I echoed.

A ray of hope lit up in my eyes...I was feeling good.

There was a smile on all our faces as we stared at each other and suddenly broke into laughter.

We had reached our destination. Not a colossal achievement, I know. But a welcome one.

"So, now what?" Rohit asked.

I looked at Akriti.

"Follow me," she said.

Whatever was to happen, it would not be the end of us or our friendship.

We then proceeded to go up the rock hill wall using the stairs carved at the side of the hill. After reaching the top, we went down the hill. To the other side.

People could be visible now. Families with curious kids smiling and laughing along with their parents. Guides talked at length with the foreign tourists. There were monkeys too.

"We can stay here for as long as we want. We just need to hide from the guards at closing time and we can practically camp here," Akriti said.

"What about food?" Rohit asked.
"There is a small restaurant down. We can eat there."
"You know that we will eventually run out of money, right?" I said.
"Yes, although I said we can stay here forever, we will move out after 3 days. By that time, R&AW would have moved their search outside the city."
"Sounds ok to me, but where will we go?"
"I have 3 days to think about it," Akriti said with a smug smile.

I shrugged my shoulders and looked around with my hands in my pockets.
"Well, let's go to the restaurant. I'm starving," Rohit said.
"Sure," Akriti said.

The food was not bad, but the menu felt more canteen-like than a restaurant. After eating, we sat at the hilltop talking and laughing. Slowly, the sun went down and the lights were starting to come up. The city on the horizon was sparkling like diamonds. But something felt off. The black sky was pertinent to my uneasiness. Everything shined a reddish yellow (shiny surfaces like rooftops of cars, bangles, mirrors, etc.) except the sky. Something else I discovered was that I could see the sky properly through the glass surfaces. Interesting, but it made no sense. The uneasiness just kept on increasing.

And soon it turned into fear.

The sky was red.

And not just red—the whole sky seemed to be a giant, distorted piece of flesh.
And then I could feel *him*.

Yes, *him*. The evil being. I can't even begin to make you understand how it felt. It was a feeling so horrifying…that…I can't explain it at all.
"Anirudh, are you alright?" Akriti asked.

I looked at her.

"You ok, bro? Another vision?" Rohit asked.

I looked at the sky. The red flesh pulsated as if blood was pumping through it.

"Anirudh, say something!" Akriti screamed, her face distressed.

I stared at her and could feel my fear spreading into her.

Then I felt some movement at the gate.

Some armed people were walking through—a man wearing a suit was in the middle. There was a terrifying aura about him. Something felt extremely wrong about him. Like he didn't belong in this world. Something demonic.

Then the man suddenly stopped. His arms rose in a bid to stop the armed men as well.

Then he slowly turned his head sideways in our direction and looked up—directly at me—and smiled.

"Run! To the forest!" Akriti screamed.

I looked at her running up ahead. Rohit looked at me with deep concern, then ran behind her.

"Come quickly, Anirudh!" Akriti screamed, looking back and running forward.

The armed men were now making their way to us.

I ran after Akriti and Rohit.

The red sky seemed to be gushing with blood. Large swaths of what seemed like a thick red liquid began to drop from the sky like waterfalls all around in the distance.

But I ignored it and ran. I tried to keep my eyes straight on Akriti's and Rohit's backs and not on the red waterfalls.

We quickly ran up the hill, down the carved stairs, across the green pasture, and into the forest.

"Keep running! I think it will take them a while to figure out that we have gone into the forest!" Akriti said.

"But where…are we going?" Rohit asked, his voice barely audible.
"Anywhere but the caves!"

Suddenly Akriti stopped. We stopped with her.

In front of us were men in armoured uniforms pointing their guns at us.

"Hands up!" one of them said.

We followed.

This was a well-planned ambush.

"No!" Akriti cried, "We are not terrorists".

I had to do something. I couldn't let them take Akriti and Rohit.

"These guys did nothing! I am the reverter! Arrest me! Let them go! Please!" I said.

Terror could be seen on Akriti and Rohit's faces as they looked at me.

"Shut up! Do as I say!" said one of the armed men.
"Slowly, lie on the ground! Get down now! Hands on your backs!"

We complied. Sweat dropped across my cheeks as my leg shuddered to go down, exhausted from all the running and walking.

We were surrounded, and there was no way to escape.

We were done.

I looked at Akriti's face to my left as we lay flat on the ground—tears filled her eyes. An unbridled sorrow had taken over her.

Rohit lay beside me to the right. He looked at me with tears in his eyes as well. It gave me a flashback of the day the bodies came back from the war.

The world was surely doomed now. I had doomed the world. All was lost.

But then I heard a voice. Along with this terrifying and gut-wrenching eeriness.

"So you admit that you are the one behind the fire and the earthquakes! Curious as to how you did it!"

I felt a sharp pain in my head—my hair was pulled to lift my head.

I saw a man squatting in front of me; his hand was entangled with my hair.

After taking a look at me up and down, he let go of my hair and my face fell to the ground with a jaw-crunching thud.

"Get up Mr Reverter!" said the man.

It was unmistakable. It was him whom I had been warned about. The evil being's presence was strong. His aura…his demeanour…words are not enough to describe the agony my heart was feeling as I looked at him.

My feet trembled as I got up, shuddering with the weight of my heavy heart.

The man smiled terrifically.

"At first I couldn't believe that it was a child that I had to target," he said, "but the more I investigated, the more I became certain that you were the one pulling the strings. The only thing I don't get is how. He never told me how you see, he told me how to find you and that you would be a threat to our nation, and he showed me a lot! A lot more than your tiny brain can handle! But maybe you can? After all, he said you are using the devil's power."

"How did you find me?" I said in a shaky voice.

He laughed, "he showed you a dream, didn't he?"

My eyes widened with fear. The dreams are connected. Too connected.

"You see, Mr Reverter, he can see every move of yours. There is a limit to how much he can tell me, but he knows that you are using the devil's powers to try to wreak havoc on this nation and the world as he told me so. He told me you would be here. He is always watching you and watching us. I didn't believe him at first, but here you are!"

"No!" I screamed. The evil being had been one step ahead of us from the very beginning. By the time I had figured out that he existed, he had already started manipulating our world.

"You are wrong! He is the one who is threatening the world. He is the devil! Not me! Don't you feel it yourself?"

"Don't you dare question him! You imbecile!"

What was I even trying to say? Devil? This was all too bizarre. It was all in vain. The evil being had completely taken over this man's thinking.

The man then grabbed my neck and started suffocating me. His eyes were filled with rage.

"Chandra! Leave him this instant!" someone shouted in the distance.

The man didn't budge. I tried to get his hands off me. But he was too strong. I couldn't breathe.

"No, sir! All devils must be killed. He has told me so! This kid will destroy not just our nation but the whole world!"

"Shekhar, stop this madman!" The chairman shouted.

My eyes began to close.

Suddenly, someone rushed in and tackled Chandra; I was released from his grasp.

But it was too late.

I fell to the ground, my eyes closed, and all went dark.

A Rogue wave

XVII

I regained consciousness and jolted up. My heart was beating fast as I gasped for air. Every breath felt like a hammer to my chest.

Flashes of that man's horridly angry face came to my mind. Just thinking about it was absurdly terrifying.

But was I dead? Where was I?

I looked around to find myself surrounded by debris. It looked like buildings were levelled by an earthquake. To my left, a lone wall rose for two stories with window openings (without any glass) that let the moonlight stream in. Sharp cylindrical iron rods protruded out of broken concrete slabs all around. Glass pieces were scattered everywhere. Debris had piled up high, and I couldn't see what was ahead. The holes in the windows only showed more rubble. I needed to get to higher ground. I needed to get to the top of the pile.

I got up slowly, careful not to place my hands on a glass piece, and tried to find a way up the debris.

This had to be that dream world. The world in which everything is connected…but how?

My breathing rate had returned to normal, along with my heart rate.

So far, I have been tossed and turned around in this dream world. And the only way to escape is to wake up in our world.

But I was either dead in our world or was in a coma. And time either doesn't exist in this world or works differently in this world. I remember having spent hours in this dream world while not even a second passed in our world; The dream at Akriti's house where we decided to start our channel.

Oh, what good did that do? Starting the channel

Climbing the concrete hill was arduous, but I reached the top. I looked around to understand where I was, but everywhere I looked, I saw a city in rubble. But there was a road down the hill — free of all destruction. So I decided to climb down and start walking forward.

Walking down the road, I shouted, "Is anyone here? Can anybody hear me?"

But of course…there would have been no one here.

The horrifying red flesh-like sky, Akriti and Rohit's crying faces and that demon on earth's vicious smile came to my mind again.

And then I stopped walking.

Anger seethed through my blood, but at the same time, I wanted to cry. The sweet face of my mom and the jolly, laughing face of my father broke me like a bittersweet symphony, each note a pang in my heart.

So I gave in and screamed in a guttural voice as tears streamed down my face.

I had had enough of this.

"Listen! I know you can hear me!"

"Leave my friends alone! Leave my world alone! Come, fight me!"

But soon all anger faded, and only a pitiful sorrow remained. I broke down to my knees and began to wail.

How the heck was I supposed to save this world? What the heck is so special about me? How am I supposed to fight this monster before me?

My friends were probably being questioned, along with my parents and their parents. Even if my friends told the truth, no one would believe them. I should have just kept quiet about my time-travelling bullcrap and just lived my remaining life peacefully

Then I heard a bell ring.

I rose and looked in the direction of the sound.

"Hello?"

The bell rang again.

"Is anyone there?"

Ting.

And I started running in that direction. It didn't seem too far.

A left turn, then a right. The bell kept ringing periodically every two seconds.

And then in the middle of an intersection filled with broken-down cars lay a single table, upon which was a golden bell. The ones you would see being used in temples.

A broad bell with a long handle at the top.

I went and picked it up. It made a metallic sound.

Then I looked around, searching for the owner of this bell.

"I know you are here! Bells don't ring themselves!"

But this was a strange world. Bells could very well ring themselves.

"Of course Anirudh, bells don't ring themselves," said a voice that I could never forget coming from behind me.

I turned around—my body shivering in fear—as I confirmed the horror before me.

It was him. The man who had tried to strangle me with his hands.

"Who are you?" I asked.

The man laughed.

"I am this 'evil being' you talk about so much," he said with a sinister smile.

I didn't know what to say. I was frozen in fear.

"Yes, I have been listening to whatever you speak. Watching every move of yours. I control this world now, and you can do nothing about it. And I will make sure you can't do anything about it. I will trap you here in this place forever."

"What is this place?" I asked, "Why me? What do you want from me?"

The man smiled and said, "Ah! How the mighty have fallen. Don't worry about it, Anirudh."

His body started becoming transparent.

"Don't worry about it."

He had disappeared completely.

Then I heard a rumbling sound along with the ground vibrating, not violently like an earthquake but more like a herd of angry bulls coming raging towards me.

But no, there were no bulls.

I could see what looked like a mountain coming closer in the distance. The sound of rumbling became louder with its approach.

But no, no mountains either.

It was water. A gigantic wave was approaching! The wave was like a blanket covering the horizon—it was big beyond belief!

I started to run in the opposite direction.

But the sound of the rumbling became louder and turned into the sound of gushing water.

I ran faster, but I wasn't fast enough. It felt like a million punches had hit me.

The water tossed and turned me. I hit debris that was now flowing along with the water like a rag doll.

Pain writhed within me, overwhelming my senses, which were already abused because of the water. But I wasn't dying. My wounds healed instantly, while I screamed incessantly. But the screaming was replaced by gurgling water as I gasped for air.
I tried to dodge the debris. However, the force of the water was too strong.

I desperately tried to dodge and tried to swim up, but each time a piece of concrete would hit me I would have to start over. All this struggle was pointless. He really did want me to be trapped here forever. I had to wake up; I needed to.

But there was no way to do that. Countless times, I told myself to wake up. All in vain.

And soon I had given up. My eyes began to close. I couldn't breathe and I couldn't take the pain anymore.

And just when I had thought that I had lost it all…Someone grabbed my hand and pulled me up with incredible speed.

Within seconds, I was out of the water and thrown onto a boat.
"Grab something! Quick!"

I responded and grabbed the edge of the bo… no, a cruiser?
The cruiser thwarted ahead. The inertia pulled me back. I lost my grip, and the force threw me onto the back of the boat.
"You alright?"
"yeah!"
"Stay there! Hold on!"

The cruiser sped on, sailed by a man who had probably saved me. I couldn't see his face as he operated the steering wheel with his back towards me.

There was water all around except for the broken shells of humanity made of concrete, that protruded out of the water like grass on arid land.

Suddenly, a guttural voice screamed, "No! You cannot leave!"

"Oh, but we can," said the sailor.

The sky turned red. The same flesh-like structure could be seen.

"Oh, this is going to be rough! If you were not hanging on to something, you should now!"

"Why?"

As if to answer my question, a huge bolt of flesh slashed the sea just ahead of us, sending a huge wave towards us. Imagine a huge human hand, but its skin is not present, and it just sent itself punching through the sea.

The sailor moved the boat to avoid it. The speed of the boat increased even more. We passed the bolt of flesh swiftly.

Another bolt thrashed right next to us. But we left it far behind. The boat was probably running at the speed of light now.

"Stop!" the guttural voice said.

More bolts tried hitting us one after the other. But they couldn't keep up with the speed of the boat.

And suddenly the boat was flying. As if it had fallen off a cliff.

I looked behind to see a plateau of water.

"Hold on!" The sailor bellowed.

A light shone from the front of the boat that was blindingly bright. And suddenly we were in a very lovely landscape.

The sky was blue. A sea of yellow flowers with a few cherry blossom trees was scattered all around.

"Brace for impact!" The man shouted.

The boat was losing altitude quickly and soon crashed into the ground.

I was thrown out of the boat. But something caught me and slowly brought me to the ground.

I looked at the boat, which was surprisingly not broken. But where was I? Where was the sailor?

"Behind you, my friend."

I turned around to see a young man smiling at me. Just looking at him somehow took all my fear and stress away.

He had a 'tika' on his forehead, the ones worn by Brahmin pandits. And was wearing a yellow shirt along with a white dhoti.

"Who are you? Where am I? Did you save me?"

"Yes, I did save you. Who am I? Just someone who loves numbers more than people and where are you? That is a bit complicated."

My eyes lit up. I could recognise his face everywhere!

"Are you Sir Srinivasa Ramanujan?"

"Yes!"

"But how?"

How was this possible? Was this really him or a figment of my imagination?

"A figment of your imagination wouldn't have been able to save you, Mr Anirudh."

I stared in awe. What was going on?

"Come with me. You should rest a bit before I answer your questions. You have had a long day."

***

"I don't know where he is, Shekhar. He or his lackeys," said the chairman.

"That's good then. He needs to stay far away from that kid," Shekhar said.
"You mean the reverter?"
"Look, I don't know why Chandra was so obsessed with killing him. But he is not some terrorist with advanced technology. Sure, something weird is happening to this kid. Just let me take over this investigation."
"I don't understand why he would just run off with the force or why they would go with him. Especially when the person he wanted to 'kill' so much is right here."
"I will figure it out. I definitely will."
"No one else is qualified…"

The chairman went into a contemplative state.
"Alright," he said after a few seconds," I have other matters to attend to. The people at R&AW and the Ministry of Home Affairs are not happy…you will now be taking over and Chandra is a wanted criminal. There is nothing I can do about that. It has been 3 hours since he escaped from the hospital. I am glad that we kept the reverter here. I am sure he is looking for him. I don't know why, but he must be. Be careful."
The chairman got up and adjusted his tie. His assistant grabbed his files.
"Thank you, sir," Shekhar said.

And the chairman left the building. The building was in a secret location unknown to most of the NIA employees.

Shekhar looked around the room: a huge glass separated the meeting room from the control room, where several people could be seen working on computers.

Shekhar then stared at the wooden round table in front of him and reminisced about his fight with Chandra.
"Stop! The Devil must die!"

Shekhar was trying his best to hold Chandra down.

"What the heck are you talking about?" Shekhar bellowed.

"He must be killed!"

Their struggle continued with Shekhar trying his best to keep him from getting up.

But Chandra managed to push him off and started running towards Anirudh's still body.

Shekhar quickly got up and threw his gun at Chandra. The gun hit the back of his head, immediately knocking him out.

"Sir, she said she is ready to talk."

The door to the control room was open, and a man was standing looking at Shekhar.

"Sir?"

"Uh…yes I will be there shortly."

"Ok, sir."

The man closed the door and left.

Shekhar got up and looked at the table once again. Chandra's rage-filled face came to his mind again.

A Valley of Flowers

XVIII

"Come along now," Mr Ramanujan said with a shy smile. I was in complete awe. This was unbelievable, yet here he was, walking before me.

After walking along for a while, we came across two bikes leaning by the flower bush to the left of the path. He picked up the bikes and rolled one towards me.

"Our destination is a little far from here," he explained.

As I pedalled along the dirt road, I looked at the surrounding scenery. The landscape was awash with vibrant shades of yellow, courtesy of the countless flowers that adorned the plain as far as you could see. The air was crisp and invigorating, carrying with it the unmistakable fragrance of petrichor.

I couldn't help but be enchanted by the delicate cherry blossom trees that were scattered along the path, their soft pink petals gently fluttering in the cool breeze. The entire landscape seemed to be alive with colour and motion, as the petals swirled and danced around me, carried along by the playful wind.

The sky above was a pure, brilliant white, casting a soft, diffused light over the entire scene. It was a peaceful, serene moment, and one that filled me with a deep sense of contentment and joy. As I gazed out at the breathtaking landscape, I knew that I was experiencing something truly special

A moment of perfect beauty and harmony that would stay with me forever.

I had forgotten how good cycling felt, how relaxing it was. I didn't know where Mr Ramanujan was taking me, but I was sure it was going to be even more mesmerizing.

"Do you see that?" He said, pointing ahead.

I could see a thatched house in the distance. As we got closer, I examined the house. It had wooden walls with lush green bushes surrounding it. Wooden pillars supported a beautifully braided straw roof that created a shade for a wooden platform in front of the house. The house looked modest, but it had a heart the size of the Pacific Ocean.

And on the wooden deck was a woman whose face lit up on seeing Mr Ramanujan.

We parked our bikes in front of the house and moved towards it. The woman came to us with a thali in her hand.

Mr Ramanujan bowed with his hand in a prayer position. A smile stretched ear to ear on his face as the woman put a tilak on his head.

He lifted his head as she was done.

"Welcome back," she said to him, looking into his eyes with pure unrequited love.

"We have a guest today, my dear Janaki," he said.

"Yes! I have prepared an extra meal!" she said, "But first," she looked at me and approached me with the thali, "I must welcome him."

She then put tilak on my head as well.

"Welcome to our humble abode," she bowed.

I smiled in delight.

"Come in! Have some food with us!" Said Mr Ramanujan.

Janaki then proceeded to open the door. An enchanting smell of food gifted my nose with a welcoming present.

And as we entered the house, I couldn't help but notice…How big it was!

I felt like I had entered a palace! How was this possible?

The ceilings were as high as a large cathedral, and the walls were adorned with beautiful artwork and photographs that depicted moments undeniably from Ramanujan's life. Interestingly, most of the photos looked like they were drone shots. The furniture was elegant and looked like it belonged in a museum.

"This was my mother's idea, not mine," Ramanujan said.

Janaki led us to the dining room, where a feast was laid out on the table.

There were bowls of steaming hot curry, plates of crispy fried snacks, and a variety of desserts that looked too pretty to eat. My mouth watered as I took in the spread before me.

"Now it is not possible for you to feel hungry in this world, nor do you need to eat anything to survive at all, but good food is fuel for the soul," Ramanujan said.

"Why?" I asked.

"Because this body of yours is not real."

What?

"Oh, don't worry about it! Eat!"

The food looked way too good. I couldn't resist it.

It was the best meal I had ever had. It reminded me of my mother's cooking. Only, the taste was somehow amplified. It brought tears to my eyes.

They were tears of joy at first, the same joy I had felt when I ate my mother's palak paneer on my first day back in 2019. But

the joy soon became bittersweet. And I couldn't help but feel awful.
The horrifying face of Chandra came to my mind, along with the crying face of Akriti as she was being held at gunpoint. I imagined the faces of my parents being interrogated.

I tried to control my tears.

But then I felt warm hands wrap around me in a hug - it was Ramanujan.

"It will be alright," he said.

I burst into tears.
Ramanujan held me tightly as I cried. He didn't say anything else, but his comforting presence was enough to ease some of the pain I was feeling.

All of this had been too much. Seeing the black sky every day had broken me. I at least had Rohit to keep me sane, but in that desolate world that Ramanujan rescued me from, I had no one.

Eventually, I pulled away from him, wiping my tears with the back of my hand. I tried to compose myself, but my voice still came out choked. "I'm sorry," I said. "I don't know what to do."
"I know, and don't worry! I will help you. We will figure it out! Right, Janaki?"
Janaki nodded.
"It will all be ok," She said.
"Thank you," I said.
"Alright, you should go get freshen up! We have lots of work to do!"
Ramanujan took me to a room on the first floor which had some new clothes on a freshly prepared bed.
"The bathroom is that way," he said pointing to a wooden door at the corner of the room.

"Come downstairs when you are done. You can try lying down on the bed if you want to, but you won't be able to sleep,"
"I'll be down soon," I told him, and he left the room.
I dropped on the bed. It was relaxing and soft. I felt good.
I tried to go to sleep but I just couldn't so I just lay there with my eyes closed for a while. After feeling rested I went and freshened up and changed my clothes.
The clothes consisted of a royal blue kurta along with a dhoti.
Would changing clothes here also change my clothes in the real world? I wondered.

***

"Of course not," replied Akriti.
"Lemme repeat the question for you once again," Shekhar said.
"Are you a part of the terrorist organization known as 'The Reverter'?"
"Of course not," Akriti repeated with the straightest face possible.
"Alright..." he said, writing something down in his notepad, "Were you in Paris on the day of the fire in Notre Dame?
"This is ridiculous!"
"More ridiculous than Anirudh being a time traveller?"
"Oh, you know that I was in school! There are attendance records. You must have checked them!"
"Where is the equipment you used to communicate with?"
"Communicate with him?"
"The members of your organization?"
"The members of...will you listen to me?!"
"Please keep your voice down."
"Take me back to the cell if you don't want to listen. I am tired of this bullshit."

Shekhar tossed his notepad aside and leaned back in his chair. He smiled at Akriti.
"What?" she said, her tone indicating her annoyance.
"I was right."
"About what, Shekhar?"
"You are not lying."
Akriti stared at him in confusion.
Shekhar got up from his chair and started pacing around the room.
"This means that you have gone crazy," he said, "or Anirudh really is a time traveller…or so he believes. This could also mean that you simply ended up believing him and Anirudh is the crazy one."
"But his predictions…"
"Could be very good bluffs. Moreover, his predictions have not always been right, have they?"
Akriti was silent.
"You said he described having these weird dreams and also seeing that the sky was red and then black after a few days, which none of you saw."
"Yes but, some of his predictions were very specific. Way too specific to be just a guess."
"Akriti, you were also undercover at the hospital. Am I right?"
"Yes,"
"What did the reports say about him?"
"He shows exceptional mathematical and analytical cognition, along with a terrifically good photographic memory."
"Could he have made up everything after analysing a lot of things? And he is suffering from schizophrenia?"
"Maybe, but his predictions were way too specific and way too…
"

"Or is he a time traveller?"
Akriti was silent.

Shekhar was also silently staring at Akriti, trying to decipher her expressions.

But then he spoke.

"The correct answer is…"

Akriti looked at him with her eyebrows raised.

"That he is a time traveller."

Akriti was completely confused by his comment.

"You see, the more I think about it, the more nothing seems to make sense."

"Except for the fact that Anirudh is a time traveller?"

"Yes!"

Akriti stared at him with an annoyed expression and then said, "Which is what I have been trying to tell you!"

"I know! But no one else is trying to understand! No one wants to believe that… I mean, even I don't want to believe it still. But this is the reasoning everyone is giving, but I know there is something way more strange going on."

Shekhar started pacing around the room faster.

"It's 23rd November today, and we have received intelligence about a viral pneumonia being spread in the Hubei province in China."

Akriti's eyes widened. "It's just like Anirudh said!" she said.

"I mean, it could still very well be a coincidence…but like you said…way too specific. But there is something else that nobody has absolutely any explanation for. Those emf outbursts."

"Right, they were observed each time we uploaded, right?"

"Now, they only last for a few milliseconds, but we used to believe that they were a form of communication between the members of the Reverter. But we are still observing these bursts even after we have supposedly caught the 'mastermind'..."

"So these fluctuations were observed in the near-infrared range?"

"Yes. The first one was the biggest and was observed only in Mumbai on the 5th of April this year."
"That is the date Anirudh said he came to 2019!"
"Huh…"
Shekhar had stopped pacing and was now looking at the screen in deep thought.
"It will take a genius to figure it out," Akriti said.
"We need to wake Anirudh up…I mean, he is in a coma…" Shekhar said.
"Do you know about Doctor Shishir?"
"Ah, that doctor of the hospital you were posted in?"
"Yes."
"Do you want me to bring him here?"
"Yes."
"You know Akriti, I have read his reports and I think the doctors here are more than capable of handling the situation following those reports."
"I know that."
Akriti and Shekhar were now locked in a staring competition.
An awkward silence ensued.
And soon, Shekhar had lost.
"Fine, I'll see what I can do."
"Will you uncuff me now?"
"I wish I could."
He then left the room, leaving Akriti dejected in her chair.
But he very well could remove the cuffs. He was now the head of this investigation, after all. Or so Akriti thought.

Red Blossoms

XIX

"I have a lot of questions," I said.
"I am sure you do," Ramanujan said.
"First, what is this place?"
"Well, you can say that this is a three-dimensional space within a higher-dimensional plane, but not exactly either."
"I don't completely understand you."

Ramanujan then took a piece of paper from a table in front of us.

The place where we were discussing was a weird one. It was like a forest inside a classroom with wooden chairs that we were sitting on. Trees covered the ceiling with their canopy, and concrete walls wrapped around their trunks. The opposite could also be seen. I don't know how we got here…but I didn't care.
"Look at this dot," he said, showing me a singular dot in the middle of the paper, drawn using a pencil.
"This dot has zero dimensions. If there was a creature living in this dot, it would be something like a tree. It would not be able to move or grow at all. It might not even be alive, but let's ignore that…now…"

He proceeded to draw a line over the dot.
"Now this line has one dimension," he said.
"Now the creature can move along the x-axis," I said.

"Yes! And now this whole paper has two dimensions! And if I stack a bunch of papers together, I get a book which has three dimensions!"

"And if we stack a bunch of books together…"

"Yes, but 'stacking' here has a different meaning. With each increase in dimension, we added a new way for our creature to move in."

"Doesn't that mean that all dimensions exist 'upon' each other? Then how can this world exist?"

"It can exist because of us humans."

I was even further confused.

"Now I don't know how. I am not one for proof or reasoning. But what I do know and understand is that all living things are projections of a higher dimension."

"So we simultaneously exist in all dimensions?"

"Precisely. I have no way of proving this. But I know it. The knowledge came to me, just like my numbers. Or at least my brain understood it in a way we don't understand. We humans severely underestimate what our brains can do."

Mr Ramanujan smiled while staring at the paper.

"The world you see around you is my creation. It exists because of me. It exists inside me. It exists all around the real world. Or 'upon' each other, as you like to call it."

I was beginning to understand what he was saying, but it felt more like a hunch. As if the answer was just within my reach, but I was falling short of grabbing it.

"Who are you? Really? You can't be Ramanujan. He is not alive."

"Oh, I am alive. And I am Srinivasa Ramanujan."

"Huh? But you died in 1920."

He smiled.

"Do you think you are still in 2019?" You are no longer there! You are in 1917!"

Suddenly, the world around us changed. We were standing at a port with a vast behemoth of an ocean in front of us. The skies were clearer than the clearest sky I had seen in my whole life. Seagulls gave their caws as they flew above my head.

A ship was being unloaded to my right by some soldiers. Some cartons said, "To His Holiness King George V."

I couldn't help but notice some soldiers wearing a red uniform. They didn't look Indian and were wearing the British flag on their uniform.

I looked at Mr Ramanujan in complete dismay. He smiled at me mischievously.

Was this an illusion? Or was I really in 1917?

***

"No! That is impossible!" Shekhar screamed.

"I am not lying sir he…he just disappeared!" said a man who was sweating from head to toe. He was wearing a white coat and I presume that he was a doctor.

"But…I need to see the footage! And where is Rakesh?!"

Rakesh came running in. "Yes, sir?" He asked.

"Call security and tell them to check if they have seen someone like Anirudh! Now!"

Rakesh ran as quickly as he heard that.
"You come with me!" said Shekhar to the baffled doctor.
Shekhar and the doctor went to see the CCTV footage of the room I was being kept in.

The doctor and I were visible on that screen. The doctor was looking at the medical monitors while I lay motionless on a white hospital bed.

Suddenly, a bright flash erupted, blinding the camera and turning the screen into a white mess.

The screen returned slowly to its normal state…you could see the absence of something on the bed.

The doctor could be seen on the screen. His hand was on his chest. And he was breathing heavily.

Shekhar turned from the screen to look at him. He was in a state of pure terror.

Shekhar left him standing there and immediately went towards the main gate to the room.

But the gate burst open with Rakesh flying in.
"We're under…" he said, but he wasn't able to finish his sentence.

Red spots bloomed from his body. Loud bangs echoed in the room along with a pandemonium of bullets.
Shekhar immediately took shelter under a desk.
"Where is he!?" said an awfully familiar voice as the commotion of the bullets halted.

A stream of blood flowed in front of a hiding Shekhar, and an ostentatious fear gripped him. He was unable to move or say anything.

It was him: Chandra. But how did he find this place?

"What did you do to him?! Shekhar?!" said Chandra, his voice sounding more guttural than before.

Shekhar knew that he had to do something. But what and how? Why was he in so much fear? Was he scared of Chandra? No, that couldn't be it. But what was holding him back?

"I can't feel him anymore, Shekhar!" his voice sounded closer. His footsteps grew louder. "I don't want to hurt you!" he said.

"Then why did you shoot up the whole place?" Shekhar thought.

Shekhar could see his feet slowly creeping up towards him.

Shekhar was now shaking.

The feet got closer.

And closer.

But then they stopped.

"What? Where did he go? What is this video?" he said.

Suddenly, the desk that Shekhar was hiding under had been blown off.

"Tell me, Shekhar!" said a demonic voice coming from the husk of a Chandra.

Shekhar tried scooting back slowly. He wasn't thinking of crawling back, but his body was moving on its own.

"Where did Anirudh go?" He screamed angrily. Then he smiled, "Oh, you don't actually know, do you?"

Chandra squatted down in front of Shekhar and started caressing his face.

"Oh! How wondrous you look, my friend! I love it!"

"What...what do you want?" said Shekhar in a trembling voice.

Chandra got back up again and started laughing maniacally. His laughter bounced across the wall, making it seem louder than it actually was.

"Nothing! But let me tell you that your dear Anirudh has abandoned your world. He has run away!"

Chandra burst into the most sinister laughter again. It didn't even sound human anymore.

"Let's go, boys! We have the world to rule!" said Chandra to the soldiers he had brought with him.

Shekhar watched Chandra leave through the door as he slowly came to his senses.

"What overtook him?" He thought to himself as he surveyed his surroundings.

"How had Chandra become like this? Had Anirudh left this world? What did that even mean?" Shekhar thought.

All of his team members were dead. Deep black blood splattered all around the walls along with the remains of what used to be his comrades. The air reeked of gunpowder. The sheer destruction was nothing short of a bomb being blasted inside the room.

"Hello? Shekhar?" A muffled voice could be heard from the back of the room.

It was Akriti. Shekar quickly manoeuvred to the room she was being kept in and opened it.

Akriti emerged, looking deeply concerned.

"Was that Chandra?" She asked.

"We need to get Rohit and leave immediately."

"Ok, but…"

Shekhar turned and started walking away. "Don't stare too long please," he said.

But how couldn't she? She knew almost everyone here.

Everyone who was now dead.

"Where is my dad?"

"Don't worry, he is not here. Now come quick."

Akriti took one last look, wiped her tears and moved ahead. Making sure that Rohit and Anirudh were fine was more important.

Rohit was being kept in another room outside the entrance. So Shekhar walked outside the door and Akriti followed.

Rohit was sleeping soundly.

"Did you sedate him?" Akriti questioned.

"No," Shekhar replied. He then grabbed a bottle near a desk beside the bed Rohit was sleeping on and sprinkled some water on his face to wake him up.

"What? Huh?" Rohit woke up, startled.

"We need to go," she said.

"So we are free?" he asked.

"Doesn't matter," Shekhar said, "Let's not waste time. Come quickly."

And they moved out of the room.

As they had almost reached the main building exit, Akriti asked a question Shekhar dreaded to answer, "And what about Anirudh?"

Shekhar stopped and slowly turned back to face Akriti.

But he just stared at Akriti, not knowing what to say. So Akriti assumed the worst, covered her mouth and started crying. She slowly fell to the ground using the wall as a crutch.

"What is going on?" Rohit asked visibly confused.

"Oh no! He is not dead!" Shekhar screamed realising his mistake.

Akriti stopped crying immediately and stared at Shekhar in confusion.

"Can someone please explain to me what the hell happened?" Rohit said.

"Wait right here," Shekhar said as proceeded to go back up to the bloody room.
Rohit looked at Akriti for an answer, but she ignored him.

And soon Shekhar came back with an open laptop in his hand, "Watch this," he said as he gave Akriti the laptop. Rohit crouched down to take a look as well.

Both of their eyes went wide as they saw the end of the footage.
"What? Did he just disappear like that?" Akriti asked.
"Yes," Shekhar replied, to their dismay.

A Brief Moment of Peace

XX

"It was the only way to save you," Mr Ramanujan said, "the way I understand it is that all of us have a specific period of influence."

I was even more confused. A cool breeze blew across my face as I stared at the deep blue ocean. Horns of the ships blew in the distance.

"What do you mean 'us'?" I asked.

He smiled and said, "Well, people like you and me!"

My eyes widened. Could I do what he did? He had created a dream world and rescued me from my world. Does he mean I can do that too? And there are more people like…us? Was the place where I met that evil being, something like Mr Ramanujan's dream world?

"So…what are we? What can we do? What do you mean by 'period of influence'?"

"As I said, all living things are projections of higher dimensions. But some beings can exist as lower-dimensional beings in higher dimensions using the real world as a platform. I haven't been able to figure out how, but I know this is possible since I am such a being. These beings can exert a certain influence over the world or the specific period of time they lived in. Based on what I have experienced we can even 'see' periods beyond our lower dimensional existence. That is how I knew about your existence and of others. But I have also realised that very few of these beings are aware of the existence of others…but that has changed ever since you travelled to 2019."

My eyes widened. I couldn't believe what he was saying yet, I felt that it was true.

"Ever since I travelled back to 2019? Didn't you go back to your own time period as well? Aren't we here in 1917 because you travelled back in time?"

"It is not what you did, but how you did it. Every being uses the fourth-dimensional world they exist in as a way to go around places within their time period, and this is the very reason (the fact that they can only move around within the time that they lived in) that they are unaware of the existence of other beings like us. But since you travelled back in time using the concept of time crystals, it sent a message across all dimensions. You had turned the clock of the whole universe backwards!"

I stared at the sea. The realisation of this all was mind-boggling. How did I do it? How was this possible?

Then another thought struck my mind.

"But if you can only exert influence in the time period of your…say, mortal existence, then how did you bring me here? Wouldn't that be impossible from your theory? And since we can only turn the whole universe backwards…or forwards..er..Using time crystals…How did you rescue me?"

"It's quite often that what you think is impossible becomes possible…for me, I knew I had to save you, so I did whatever I felt I could, I tried reaching out to your world and it worked! I don't know how, but it feels like something helped me to get you. That same something that has guided me all my life, with all my numbers and equations. It is also my theory that the 'message' that was sent across space-time when you reversed the state of the whole universe, might have something to do with it…but anyway, it's a

shame I couldn't give out more to the world, but it seems you can! You somehow discovered a way to interact with the time crystal of the whole universe! You can save the world from...that being."
"But how?!"

I shouted a little too loud. People glared at us with suspicion.

"It's best if we go somewhere quiet, come with me," Sir Ramanujan said.

Houses passed, horse carts rode around and soon the path became less trodden as we entered a more vegetated area. As we journeyed on, the number of houses dwindled and the sound and sightings of horse carts became even less prevalent. Before we knew it, our path had transformed into a less-trodden trail that led us into a dense, forested area.

"Isn't this quiet enough? There is no one here."

"There is a certain place I wanted to show you. It's a place I regularly visited as a child."

As we ventured deeper into the forest, a magnificent Brahma temple emerged before us. The temple stood tall, crafted using shining white marble. Every step of its roof tower was adorned with intricate sculptures. At the entrance, a small pond welcomed us, its surface blanketed by mesmerising lotus flowers.

"This is beautiful!" I exclaimed.

"I used to come here quite often," he said.

There were only two or three people around. The place was in stark contrast to the busy port we had come from.

"Let's go inside," he said.

The inside was even more mesmerising. The temple was a large hall with clay pot lamps on all walls. The room was mostly dark except for the Idol in front of us and the small amount of light that the deepaks gave. The whole temple seemed to be in a different world altogether; an ethereal existence in a world full of chaos.

"I think it is Lord Brahma who has guided me. It is he, the creator, the one true Truth in this world."

"I had a dream, in which there was a being who told me to stop, or the world would end, I knew it was not the evil being who has been tormenting us. In another dream, that being said that it is dying and 'he' is coming, I must race. The being also said that I am the only one who can save the world. Then in another dream, where I was being tormented by the Evil being, a big wall of light pushed me into Akriti's dream. Could that be Brahma? And is he dying?"

Sir Ramanujan looked concerned.

"It can't be Brahma, but it is a possibility. But we know what we need to do."

"What?"

"We have to stop this evil being."

I mean…yes of course.

"Can you tell me about him? Do you know anything?"

"I don't know much, but he doesn't seem to be of human origin."

"Then what is he?" He stared at the Idol for some time. He seemed to be thinking deeply, sweat dripped across his face. Concern had overtaken his face.

"I do not know," he said. His gaze still focusing on the Idol.

"But you know what Anirudh?" he said as he turned to face and placed his hands on my shoulders, "We have you!" A big smile filled his face.

I started laughing. I knew nothing about what to do, yet the whole world seemed to be at the mercy of me figuring out what I needed to do.

But I was done standing still. I had to do something, and I was determined to do it.

"So what should I do?"

"Do you remember anything after the time you died in that blast?"

"All I remember is feeling serenity and weightlessness, and then slowly feeling heavy again, and then I was in 2019."

"Trust me when I say, that more happened when you died than you remember. We simply need to unlock that part of your memory."

"Ok, but how will we do that?"

"You will seek enlightenment."

Enlightenment? Is he serious?

"You see what has happened is that you saw something like the singularity, I know that I did."

"Singularity, as in the point of extreme mass density at the centre of a black hole?"

"Yes, but I meant more of the mathematical singularity, a place where mathematics misbehaves. All known laws of physics just don't matter. A black hole is a naked singularity…my point being, that you saw a singularity, analysed it, and did something amazing with it. But your mind had shut those memories off for some reason."

"And what does enlightenment have to do with it?"

"Enlightenment is simply a process of knowing oneself and our place in it. Enlightenment is also something that physicists have been chasing for a long time to achieve. A grand unified theory, that explains everything in the universe. Some humans gained this knowledge and became beings like us. Some even made complete religions out of it and performed miracles, but even they hit a wall with the number of powers they have, and the amount of influence they have, and they referred to this wall as Truth. Brahma, 'God' that Christianity and Islam talk about, Nirvana and the four truths In Buddhism, are all the same things. You have met the truth, and the truth has helped you. All you need to do is look within yourself and find it."

My gaze went towards the idol of Lord Brahma. I was shivering. The whole world seemed to be caving around me. I knew what I needed to do, but it was scary. My whole life had led me to this moment. And the path ahead was now clear.

"Meditation," I said.

"Yes, but it won't be easy. We are talking about extreme dedication, and focus. For who knows how long."

"I am ready."

"Then let's go back to my world."

And with that, we were back in a world full of yellow flowers and cherry blossom trees all around. Mr Ramanujan showed me a particular tree. A nice wooden platform was made for me to sit on with the tree as my backrest. The tree itself was a sacred fig, a species of fig native to the Indian subcontinent and Indochina region.

"Your physical body doesn't exist here, so you won't feel hungry or tired. Just try not to fall asleep and keep your mind free of thoughts. Do what the Buddha did."

To meditate is to decrease the level of activity of the mind and to increase the level of consciousness. The Budha meditated every day to achieve complete consciousness. And I had never once meditated in my whole life. This was going to be quite a challenge. But I was not going to give up. I didn't know how the answer was going to come to me, But I knew that it was. All I needed to do was start my meditation and clear my thoughts.

So I sat on the platform. For the last time, I looked at the vast land. The vast horizon before me seemed to smile at me.

"Now then, I shall leave you be," said Ramanujan as he turned and walked away. I watched him slowly disappear on the horizon. And he was gone.

I turned back to see the Horizon. The flowers sway rhythmically with the wind. The temperature was cool, and all was calm. It was now time to begin.

So I closed my eyes and closed the door to my thoughts.

Increasing Chaos

XXI

"Yes, I am absolutely fine, Mom," Rohit said, talking on the phone. "Anirudh…is also good!....yes, yes…I will talk to you soon…What tall creatures? I can't hear you properly. Don't worry, we will talk soon. Bye!"

Rohit cut the call and returned the phone to Shekhar, who kept it inside the dashboard drawer of the car.

Akriti was staring out the window with her face incredibly dull. Slowly she watched the trees go by one by one, and the slow-moving mountains that covered much of the horizon.

"It will be alright, Akriti," Rohit said.

There was no response from Akriti. Her spirit had been drained.

Rohit looked at her plaintively, he knew that she was in pain. More and more of the things that went wrong had made Akriti forlorn. Rohit wanted to cheer her up, but there was nothing that he could do that would make Akriti smile.

Or was there?

"You know Anirudh has a huge crush on you?"

Akriti immediately turned around and glared at Rohit. Shekhar swerved and almost ran the car into a ditch.

"I am not lying!"

"Oh! Shut up, Rohit! He knows that I am much older than him!"

"Oh, he only knows that now! For a long time, he believed you to be 15! Also, should I remind you that he is 21?"
"But..." Akriti started blushing. "I don't think he will be happy that you told me!"

Yeah! I am not amused!

"So? Do you like him?"

"No! Not like that!"

Right...

"Ok, I was lying," Rohit started laughing.

"Oh, you gobblehead!" Akriti screamed as she threw a small back pillow at Rohit.

I don't think she believed him in the first place, but the doubt was placed in her head, do I like her? Or do I not?

But it did improve her mood. Rohit's plan worked.

"Don't do that again..." Akriti said as she went to look out the window.
"But you love him, right? As a friend, I mean," Rohit asked.

Akriti turned back and looked at him with no expression as if she was contemplating about what to say, but before Rohit could get confused, "Of course!" Akriti said with a big, heartwarming smile.

Rohit smiled back.

"I hope he comes back soon," Akriti said.

"I am sure he will," Rohit assured.
Suddenly, something dropped with a loud thud just a few metres before the car. Shekhar quickly applied the brakes to stop the car. But it was too late, the car was going to hit it.

But the thing moved, and the car was saved from crashing. Shekhar got out of the car as soon as it stopped. Rohit and Akriti followed.

A tall figure slowly moved ahead into the forest to their right. Something huge and metallic. It looked like a mosquito but with skinny legs and a huge bloated body. It was as tall as the Eiffel Tower. Thin wires were protruding from its head like the antennas of an ant.

"This is exactly the thing Anirudh saw in his first dream!" Rohit screamed.

"Yes! This looks exactly like what he described!" Akriti said.

Other cars had also stopped as people stared at the immense monstrosity, moving ever increasingly ahead.

But they heard another rumbling sound from behind them. Everyone turned around.

The road they were on was surrounded by forest on both sides. Trees were falling in a straight line.

Things that looked like gigantic black centipedes emerged from the forest at the end of the line.

"Inside the car! Now! We gotta go!" Shekhar said as he ran back to the car. Rohit and Akriti followed.

The centipedes screeched and started slowly moving towards them. They were as tall as a two-story building, as wide as a bus, and up to 20 feet long. Dark, ravenous teeth covered their mouth.

The engine revved, and the car sped off.

But movement could be seen in the trees ahead.

And another centipede came out in the front.

It withered towards their car, smashing other cars in its way. Shekhar didn't know what to do.

And as if coming to his rescue, a plane crashed into the centipede ahead. A huge blast ensued, pushing the centipede out of the road.

What's worse is that it was a passenger plane.

Rohit stared in horror as the car went along the upturned creature. Smoke ran all around. Fire seemed to dance with a deathly stare across the forest.

Shekhar quickly called the chairman and put his phone on the speaker. He then swiftly kept it on the dashboard.

"Yes? Shekhar? I was just about to call you," said a raspy voice.

"Sir! You won't believe what we just saw!"

"I know it's all over the news. Those tall metallic creatures match Anirudh's descriptions exactly. And you might not know, but they have appeared all around the world. And not just the tall metallic things, but those strange snake-like creatures too."

"Everywhere?"

"Yes!"

Shekhar looked into the rear-view mirror to see the centipede behind him. It was quite far now. Several cars were speeding past him or were behind him. It was extremely chaotic.

The chairman continued, "You need to get to the headquarters as soon as possible! The police will try to control the situation now, but the military is being dispatched as we speak! The sheer number of these things is worrying! Soon there will be a nationwide curfew!"

"Oh God! But we are currently being chased by one of those creatures! Where is the military?"

"Where are you?"

"We just left the base."

"How fast is the creature moving?"
Shekhar looked in the rear-view mirror again. Akriti and Rohit turned around as well.
"Very slowly, I barely see it now."
"This is an unprecedented disaster! the military is neither ready nor anywhere near. Again, the sheer number of these things is gonna make it extremely difficult to do anything."
"This is unbelievable! Is there any news on Chandra? Is this his doing?"
"We don't know if he caused this, but we have his location and a task force covering the perimeter. You need to get here quickly, but you can't take flights as they have been suspended because of the tall mosquitoes and the creatures. You know what? I want you to drop Akriti and Rohit off at their homes and head to a helicopter pad nearby. Message me when you get there, and I will dispatch a helicopter to get you. Understood? And tell everyone to stay in their homes and not to move out for any reason whatsoever!"
"All clear!"
"Great! Be safe! Hurry!"

The phone was hung up.

"I hope you understand Akriti," Shekhar said
"No! I want to be with my dad!"
"Currently, you are a civilian, and we can't…"
"I am a trainee agent working under R&AW!"
"I know you are, but honestly, you wouldn't be of much help. I also feel that if there is a slight chance that Anirudh comes back, he will go to his home, and someone should be there when he does."
Akriti wanted to retaliate, but she bit her lips and sighed. The weight of truth had dawned on her. She looked back at the barely visible centipede.

"You…are right…I wouldn't be of much help…I do hope Anirudh comes back and we are there when he does. I am sure he will come right home," she said.
"Good. You are a phenomenal girl, Akriti!"
"But what if Chandra comes looking for Anirudh when he comes back?" Rohit asked.
"You heard the chairman, right? It looks like we know where he is and we will be taking care of him."
"Did you see those creatures just now? Do you really think a small task force would be enough to handle him and his army?"

Shekhar had seen a little more than just a gigantic creature. He had seen the rage-filled and deranged eyes of Chandra. He had heard his ferocious laughter as it echoed along the walls of the blood-painted room.
"I think your silence says a lot," Rohit said.
"Just trust me," Shekhar said.

Rohit laid his head on the window and looked out the window in disbelief at the world he was in. Akriti, too, went back to a dejected state. Angry that she was not allowed to do anything. "What were these creatures? Was Anirudh safe?" Akriti thought.

***

In front of me lay countless sheets of paper at least a meter long. The sheets stretched across the horizon.

Sir Ramanujan was smiling at me while I looked at him, dumbfounded.

"This is way too much information!" I complained.

"It is what it is. Did you think data from a singularity would be any less?"

"But this isn't even half of it!"

Some of my memories had returned from my encounter with the singularity and, along with them, a huge headache.

Let's just say my brain closed off these memories for a reason.

But I had been meditating for 2 years. Earlier I couldn't concentrate for more than 4 minutes, but it gradually increased and now I can concentrate for two days straight.

I started by focusing on just my breathing and trying to have no thoughts, then I moved on to focusing on my internal processes. It was weird enough that I could sense everything around me, and now I could focus on even the smallest of changes around me and within me.

My memory capabilities had increased significantly. Now I could not only see the memories of each part of my life, but experience it as if I was living it.

But there was a noticeable hole in my memory. A hole that was quite big yet refused to be filled.

But just today, while exploring the memories of my last few minutes in 2025, I remembered the first few seconds of my encounter with the singularity. After I had died, I came in contact with the singularity. And with it came an enormous amount of just pure information.

Imagine floating on a vast pool of water, and above you is a large white sphere in a dark sky. The sphere is talking to you somehow. You don't understand how something that doesn't have a mouth can speak, but it does. And you feel the most inconspicuous feeling of love in your heart, another feeling that I cannot describe. The feeling is…good…but I cannot put it into words.

This is what I saw and felt, but I couldn't concentrate anymore and the information that the sphere gave me was way too much for me to understand and I had completely lost focus. I opened my eyes to see Sir Ramanujan smiling as he showed me those sheets of paper lying all around.

"This, Anirudh, is enough for you to understand one simple thing. You can do the same things I do."

"How? I can't even read one word on these papers! And there are thousands of them!"

"Then let me make a computer for you."

All the papers were now lifted in the air. Slowly, they started flying towards each other and started to converge into a ball above Sir Ramanujan.

With a bright flash, the ball of paper turned into a laptop. The laptop slowly came down and rested on my lap.

"Wow," I said.

"Well, now you have all the information as files inside the computer."

"Ok, this does make it easier to read, but how do I still read them?"

"Open up a file."

I went into the folder labelled '1' out of the hundreds of folders on the desktop.

Inside were 50 files. I opened the first file.

And inside the file were…numbers. The numbers were separated by commas like a CSV file.

But then I noticed that the numbers followed a pattern. It was the Fibonacci series! But only up to the 5th line.

"What is this?"

"Therein lies the answer to how you can try to teleport."
"What nonsense!"
"Just keep analyzing."

And with that, he disappeared.

I sighed and got to work. The fate of the world depended on me after all…

And so I sat for 3 days, seeing the numbers file after file. Until I realized what these numbers really meant.

These were a sort of log of the energy transactions across the whole universe.

And that is when I realized how I could teleport and how Sir Ramanujan had managed to teleport.

It is a simple transaction of energy between the higher dimensions and our third dimension. Since we have access to matter through the higher dimensions, we could initiate this process of exchange of energy.

Just as we could ignite a fire using a piece of wood and air, providing enough energy for oxidation to occur. Wood and air are two different states of matter yet they come together to make a fire.

Similarly, the 4th and the 3rd dimension come together to enable teleportation. The only thing you need is energy, and well access to the higher dimensions, which we possess.

"It has taken me a long time to figure this out, but this is how I brought you to my world and 1917."

"Even so, how do I have this 'reaction' occur?"
"Let's first go back to 1917. Where my body exists."
"Where your body exists! That's it! That is the reason you can't go very far into the past or the future, since you don't have matter in

that part of higher dimensions since your body exists in only the period of your life!"
"Yes! Let's go."

And with that, we were back in the Brahma temple.
"I got it exactly right this time!" Sir Ramanujan exclaimed in excitement.
"What?"
"The energy calculations for our energy transactions to take place. Some mistakes can end up having us teleport underwater or even underground."

I understood what he was talking about. I also understood that I would have to go through a ridiculous amount of calculations just to perform a simple teleportation.

And with that began my year-long practice of learning how to manipulate using the higher dimensions. After about 6 months, I no longer needed to go to the 4th dimension as I had learned how to keep a part of my consciousness in the higher dimension. It was only through more meditation that I unlocked more memories and more 'conversations' with the singularity that made this possible.

The only problem was the amount of calculations involved. Even after my increased mathematical capability, each calculation felt like a horribly long integral calculus question.

Appalling figures

XXII

Looking at the behemoth, Dr Rupal, the team leader of the I.S.R.O team, gaped in awe and astonishment. Never before in his whole career had he seen such a thing as this. No one had. But the more she looked, the more familiar it felt. She could almost feel like she could just figure out what it was, but logically, it could only fit inside a Hollywood action flick.

"Here are the muon tomography images of the target, Dr Rupal," said a woman, whom Dr Rupal did not recognise; she was not a part of her team.

"I am sorry, who are you?"

"Oh, forgive my manners. I am Anaika, an assistant PhD scholar to Professor Brijwal. Your PhD is in Advanced Material Sciences, am I right? You were a part of the development team for the GSLV Mark III right?"

"Well, aren't you an enthusiastic girl Anaika! Nice to meet you."

"Oh, it's an honour. Dr Brijwal asked me to give these images to you and to bring you and your team to him."

"Great, let's move then."

"Absolutely, follow me."

Dr Rupal nodded at her team, and they followed Anaika. None of the team members of Dr Rupal were assistants, let alone interns.

"Anaika must have been an excellent student," Dr Rupal thought.

The metallic monstrosity stood silently tall. Its eye was ominous, like a cyclops gazing forward with a red tint. Numerous other metallic giants were visible in the distance. Military vehicles were all around, pointing guns and missiles at the colossal metal hunks. Helicopters hovered above them regularly.

Soon, Dr Rupal and her team of four reached Dr Brijwal's cabin, which was a makeshift lab inside a shipping container. The container had two holes on top and a window on the side overlooking the metallic monstrosity.

The ones on the top had some kind of machinery on top. Dr Rupal immediately recognised them as new muon tomography imagers.

"Good afternoon Dr Rupal," said Dr Brijwal, with a sharp but fake smile. She could tell that he was rather stressed.

"Good afternoon," she replied, shaking his hand.

"If you have taken a look at the images, you would know..."

Dr Rupal opened the file containing the images and examined them.

"The creature has a completely hollow body, except for a very small point at its theoretical centre of mass," Dr Rupal explained.

"Yes, and not only that but inspect the lagrangian peeks in the graph behind the images."

Dr Rupal flipped through the images and looked at the graph in each one of them.

Her eyes widened in disbelief. She looked up towards Dr Brijwal and spoke out haphazardly.

"How is this possible? Have you verified these observations? Have you retaken the images?"

"Three times. We are doing it for the fourth time currently, but no matter what we do..."

"This amount of mass, with such density, should have created a black hole!"

"Indeed, Dr. Rupal."

The conversation was interrupted by a beep, followed by the sound of a printer. Dr Brijwal immediately turned around and ran towards the source of the sound. The beeping stopped, and he came back slowly with a piece of paper in his hand.

He appeared to be studying it carefully.

"Are those the fourth observations?"

"Yes."

"And?"

Dr. Brijwal looked up from the paper and gave it to Dr Rupal.

Dr. Rupal carefully took the images and turned them. Only to bellow out in astonishment.

"Impossible!"

Dr. Rupal's hands started shaking.

"The world is about to end," said Dr. Brijwal, his voice sounding almost like a cry.

"Any information on the organic creatures?"

"They seem to be coming from only inside the forests. We don't know what they are, but for now, the military seems to be keeping them out of highly populated areas, but only God knows what is happening to places near the forests."

"Only highly populated areas?"

Dr. Brijwal just stared. The military was doing all it could, given the situation, but there were so many of them.

A loud alarm started blaring in the camp around the behemoth.

"Everyone! Get out! Now!" Dr Brijwal screamed, grabbing his suitcase and running out. Everyone followed him immediately.

The ground was shaking now. A loud rumbling noise could be heard coming from the behemoth.

Dr Rupal turned around to look at it.

Tentacle-like wires protruding from the behemoth were moving to and fro as if they were looking for something to grab. A few of the tentacles had dug into the ground and were maybe holding the behemoth firmly to the ground.

But most of them were vibrating vigorously, stretched out like a dancing peacock's feathers. Dr Rupal looked around at the other behemoths in the distance only to find them behaving similarly.

Boom!

A helicopter hovering close to the behemoth exploded mid-air with a blindingly bright flash.

"Everyone on the ground! Cover your heads!" A soldier shouted.

Pieces of the helicopter were falling everywhere.

A beam of light emerged from the eye of the behemoths all around and converged at a point. At the point of convergence, a huge beam immediately shot to the ground sending a huge shockwave that uprooted all the trees in the vicinity and sent more debris flying around.

After everything had settled, Dr Rupal slowly got up to being helped up by a soldier.

She looked around to see if her team members were ok. She was glad to see that they were.

But then she noticed the lifeless body of Anaika lying on the ground. Her eyes were wide open and her stomach had a hole with an enormous piece of metal in it.

***

"Anirudh, something is not right with your world. "

"What do you mean?"

"I am not sure. It just feels that it is drifting away from our universe. And the drifting is spreading to other worlds as well."
"You mean other people like us? Their worlds?"
"Yes."
"It has to do something with the evil being. You said that it is not of human origin."
"Yes, I didn't feel any resemblance to any human-like qualities from it."
"Then what is it?"
"I don't know, but what I do know is that I am unable to look forward in time. It's very garbled. The time your world is a part of seems to be, as I said, drifting away. As if something is eating it."
I just stared with my eyes wide.
Ramanujan put his hands on my shoulder and said, "You must figure out how you reverted the world."
"I know…I need to bring in more of my memories back…but it's just too much information!"
Imagine reading a 500-page book every day and trying to memorise every word of it.
"Only you can save the universe from whatever that appalling figure of a living being is."

Ragnarok

XXIII

The helicopter landed on the helipad at the top of the headquarters building. Mumbai City was visible in its full glory from the top.

A man dressed in black approached Shekhar, his voice barely audible against the whirring helicopter blades.

"Good morning, sir! I am here to debrief you on the task force situation! Follow me!"

They entered the building as the man continued: "The team is standing by at the location and has it surrounded. Here is the file containing the location information and how we got it." The man handed Shekhar a file as they continued down the stairs.

The debriefer continued. "Reports of armed men entering an abandoned farmland near Alibagh were received yesterday, almost right after you called at us."

"Around 10:30 pm?" Shekhar said, looking at the photos of the land in the file.

"Yes, two people were walking by when they saw an army marching towards a house on the land. Later, a cow herder heard gunshots emanating from the land this morning. The herder had let his cows graze on the land as the land was disputed. A court case has been running for 5 years, and no one usually comes to the land except the herder."

They were on the ground floor and walking in a long corridor filled with people in shirts and pants carrying large files.
"Are those people safe?"
"The locals? Yes."
"And the task force?"
"Ready to infiltrate."

The man suddenly turned right and opened a door. He gestured for Shekhar to come in.
"Welcome, Shekhar," said the chairman at the centre of the room.

It was a large, dark room. Rows of computers were arranged to face a large projector screen at the front of the room. The screen was to the left of the door Shekhar had entered from.
"Now that you are here, you will be spearheading this operation along with Miss Smrita here," the chairman said.

Miss Smrita was at one of the computers and stood up as soon as the chairman addressed her. She bowed slightly to Shekhar and Shekhar did the same.
"The goal of this mission is simple," the chairman continued. "Capture Chandra alive or…eliminate him if capturing is not possible."
"Understood," Shekhar said.
"You know Chandra the most out of anyone in the whole division, I am sure you could talk to him and convince him,"
"The Chandra we knew is gone."

The chairman gave a sorrowful nod and put his hand on Shekhar's shoulder.
"Then you know what you should do," he said.

Shekhar looked as firm as ever and said, "It is something I must do."

"Well then, I must go. I have a meeting with the prime minister regarding the sudden emergence of those creatures."

"Good luck, sir," Shekhar said.

The chairman said with a titter, "Good luck to you too Shekhar."

As he made his way towards the door, bodyguards emerged from the walls like ghosts and followed him.

But just as he was going to turn the handle, he stopped and turned back slowly.

After staring at Shekhar for three seconds, he said, "And don't hesitate to fall back."

The projector screen displayed four camera views: one from the captain of the Alpha team, and one from the chieftain of the Beta team was an aerial view. The other was a thermal view from the side of the building.

"Team Alpha is good to go," said the captain.

Shekhar adjusted his earpiece to hear him better.

"Drone is ready," said Miss Smrita. Shekhar nodded.

"Head to the back door, team Beta standby at the front," said Shekhar.

"Team Alpha moving in," said the captain.

"Team Beta standing by," said the chieftain.

"I want drone 2 to track Team Alpha," said Shekhar.

Smrita nodded, and another window popped up on the screen.

The tall field grass gently swayed with the wind as the captain moved forward along the sidewall of the building. The atmosphere was eerily silent.

The building was a two-storey one with a balcony at the front and a conical roof. There were two windows, one at the front and one at the right side of the building. Team Alpha had decided to move to the back from the left side to avoid an ambush from the windows.

"Requesting status of the backyard from the drone," said the captain as he stopped the team just at the corner of the backside. The officers stood attentively, with guns pointing ahead.

Shekhar looked at the projector screen, but the drone footage showed no movement.

"All clear, proceed to the door," he said.

The team then moved forward, slowly. After reaching the door, the captain slowly checked if the door was open.

And it was.

The captain motioned one of the officers to kick open the door while he would cover it, pointing his gun straight at the door.

Just like they had trained, another officer took position to his left while the officer was ready to open the door.

"Now!" said the captain.

Immediately, the door burst open, and the team moved in. Very meticulously, the team of six officers pointed their guns in each direction.

"Backroom clear, moving into the hallway."

The officers moved into the hallway in a line with the captain at the front. Each room along the hallway was burst in with two officers guarding both sides of the hallway.

But there was no one there.

"Ground floor clear, moving to the first," said the captain.

"Copy that."

The thermal imaging was already showing a group of people in the centre of the house. According to the construction plan retrieved from the building permit office archives, the house only had two floors, and since the ground floor was cleared, the moment of truth lay on the first floor.

The slow creaking of the wooden stairs and the absence of any other sound made the captain uneasy. But the mission had to go on. There was no other way to understand what was going on.

The first floor only had two doors leading into a single large room.

"Team Alpha requesting status inside the room."

"Team Beta, move in. Standby at the stairs. Thermal imaging shows 4 bogeys inside the room in front of the first door," said Shekhar.

"Team Beta moving in."

"Team Alpha, move in when team Beta is in position. Any further requests?"

"No."

The ground floor resonated with the sound of a door opening.

"Team Beta is in position."

The captain of team Alpha firmly held the doorknob in the front. He motioned three of the officers towards the second door.

They all nodded, and the door was opened.

The room was big and had two windows, one to the front and the other to the left. A man was sitting on a chair looking out the large window. Two armed soldiers stood on both sides of the man. A body was hung from the top of the conical ceiling inside a body bag.

The team pointed their guns at the man and the two soldiers.

"Put your hands up!" The captain shouted.

The man slowly turned and looked at the captain. Then he smiled and got up from the chair.

"I am disappointed, Shekhar," said the man.

"Put your hands up now!" The captain shouted.

Chandra put his hands up, but so did the members of the team Alpha. Guns fell on the wooden floor with a crunch and a thud.

"What are you all doing? Get into position!" The captain shouted. But the officers did nothing.

"What is this?!" the captain shouted.

"You should have come to me yourself, Shekhar. I would have given you moksha."

Chandra started coming closer to the captain.

"Stand back! I will open fire! Stand back!"

Chandra smiled and slowly crept closer.

"Come here, Shekhar, and I will spare this man."

The captain fired his gun, but with a bright flash, the bullet vanished the moment it came close to Chandra.

"Fall back! Retreat! Mission Abort!" Shekhar shouted.

But it was too late. The captain suddenly turned to face the officers and fired at them before shooting himself. Blood splattered on the room walls and Chandra's face.

"Team Beta is out!"

Chandra picked up the body cam from the lifeless body of the captain and put it in front of his face.

"Don't worry, Shekhar," he said, "The whole world will receive moksha very soon anyway."

"What do you mean?"

"The world as we know it is ending. But all will be reborn. He will give us a new life!"

"Who is 'he', Chandra?"

"He is God, Shekhar. And not just any God..." Chandra started smiling like a little child, "The God of the whole world! Not just

our universe! You know Shekhar? There are worlds beyond our universe?"
"What worlds, Chandra? You need to stop this! Whatever this is! Lots of people are being killed!"
"Oh, this can't be stopped! Not after Anirudh left you all to die!" Chandra started laughing maniacally.

And with that, the camera feed was cut.

Utter silence filled the control room. Shekhar stared at the projector screen with his body frozen in fear.

2301 years

XXIV

"Are you sure, Anirudh?" Sir Ramanujan said.
"Absolutely," I said. "It has been 2301 years since I started my meditation."
"Need I remind you…"
"That time passes differently here? After all, what is time but a constant movement of energy? There is almost no exchange of energy here. Except of course—talking and walking."
"Yet, do you have all the answers? After spending 2301 years…"
"Some, yes. I at least know how you brought me here and how I reverted the whole universe."
"But that isn't enough, is it?"
Flashes of different memories of my life came to my mind, along with the fragmented memories of my encounter with the naked singularity.

For 2000 years, I have been swimming through my memory galaxy and trying to decipher the information that I could recover from bits of memories of the naked singularity.
The singularity is huge. The information is immense. And the fact that I can only remember very small fractions of having seen it is a serious issue. However, "There are still some memories left un-explored, but there is only one way to unlock them," I replied.
"To go back home," He said.
"Yes!" I replied ecstatically.

Why? Because the place is full of memories. Full of triggers that can help unlock the path to the missing memories. The very place that I landed back in 2019 could be a huge clue.

And besides, I know how to revert back the universe…I mean I know how I did it, I haven't practised it. But it is quite similar to teleportation, with added…stuff (I'll tell you soon)

Then Sir Ramanujan stretched his arms out and said, "Well then, friend! Going back won't be easy, but I know you can do this! The world…"

"Depends on me, yes yes. I have heard that a gazillion times."

Then he warmly put his hands on my shoulder and said, "Then this is goodbye."

A smile erupted on our faces, a smile of satisfaction and deep love between a master and his disciple.

"Well then, I'll make the path for you, Anirudh, The Enlightened one."

"Oh, I wouldn't call myself enlightened just yet."

And so he did.

A bright flash erupted behind me.

I turned around to see a black rectangle with the width of the India gate and a height stretching into space.

Only the rectangle wasn't really black. It was a doorway into the other world. The world that led to 2019.

"Very welcoming, isn't it?" Said, Sir Ramanujan.

"Indeed, but I'll be fine."

"Good luck!"

"Thank you!"

Because God, indeed, plays dice. And to play dice effectively, you must have luck. Luck is nothing but randomness. But this randomness is why we exist. And that is why luck is God. And I have been very lucky lately. Very lucky to be alive.

I took a step forward into the black abyss.

With one foot inside and the other back in Ramanujan's world, I turned around for a final goodbye.

Ramanujan waved at me and smiled.

I turned around and finally made the final step into the world that evil had completely taken over.

As soon as I took the step inside, the doorway immediately closed behind me.

Complete darkness ensued.

But was there anything to see? My footsteps were muffled. I could only feel the vibrations of each footstep hitting the ground. No reverberations at all.

The lack of sound was unnerving. But as if answering my question of why there was no sound, I heard a huge thud in front of me. The same noise that can be heard when huge stadium light relay switches are turned on.

But there was no bright light like there would be in a stadium, only two gigantic red eyes staring at me menacingly.

"You can't scare me anymore!" I shouted.

The eyes persisted in their staring.

"Who are you?" I shouted again.

The eyes slowly closed and disappeared.

I was left in the dark again.

But the surrounding scene started changing. Slowly, like a painter painting on a black canvas, I could see a dusk sky and some mountains rising around me. Then there was grass on the ground–green and swaying rhythmically with the wind.

Dark trees started sprouting up from the ground like earthworms and soon took all the visibility there was.

A path less trodden had formed in front of me.

"You still haven't figured it out, have you?" A voice whispered in my right ear, startling me.

I immediately turned around but found no one.

But then I noticed that the sky had started to turn black and soon, I could see the stars. The moon appeared and swam across the sky with increasing speed. Then the brightness of the sky increased until it was bright as day and soon after that, it started becoming dark again. Again, the moon sped away, bringing the sun behind it. Shadows of the trees came into existence, grew big, and died only to rise again. The moon and sun seemed to be running after each other.

The speed of the chase increased ever more until everything was a blurry mess of light and shadow. The sky became a dull white and the ground black as night. The trees had all decayed.

I was confused.

"What is this?" I shouted.

But there was no answer.

The white sky above started showing red lines. It looked like the retina of a human eye.

Soon more red lines appeared. The trees had started to develop peculiar bulges, which soon opened like eyelids, to reveal brownish eyes.

Eyes, each having a blood-red iris, stared at me. Thousands of eyes looking from all directions felt creepy beyond belief. The sky had turned entirely red.

"I know what you are trying to do, but it just won't work."

It was trying to scare me. But nothing can scare me anymore. Not after the years I spent meditating and making my mind as still as a rock.

I couldn't stand still, doing nothing, so I decided to walk along the path in front of me.

The eyes eerily followed me.

I needed to get out of here. But how? I couldn't sense any matter on Earth.

"Save me!" I heard a scream coming from behind me. It was at quite a distance, but I had to do something.

A trap? I don't care. This monster cannot scare me anymore.

"Help!" A gruelling cry could be heard from the left.

"Somebody, please help!" Another voice from the right.

Nope, definitely not actual cries for help.

Then suddenly, with a bright flash, a large screen popped in front of me. It showed tall tripod-like structures with laser beams shooting from in front of them. Then it showed destroyed buildings, and helicopters falling from the sky or busting in the surrounding sky.

Then the screens changed to show gigantic worm-like creatures moving through villages and…crushing everything in their path…even people.

Were those cries for help from actual people? Was this actually happening?

"This isn't real! You cannot scare me!"

But why was it trying to scare me so much? What was the need?

And that is when it clicked.

It was trying to keep me occupied. It was trying to stop me from thinking. Why do I think that it is trying to stop me from thinking? Because it knew that I was close to the answer. Maybe it was watching Ramanujan's world that could be why Ramanujan felt that he was losing connection to my world. This thing wanted to stop him from intervening. And stop me from progressing.

But no more. I was not going to let it win.

So I sat down, closed my eyes and focussed. How can I go back? I needed access to matter from earth in my time, but this being was stopping me from doing so.

But before I could think more, I felt like I was falling.

I opened my eyes to find myself in complete darkness again. Falling through the abyss, I felt nothing but the most unscrupulous contempt for this being.

But it won't work. I can't die in this place.

So I closed my eyes and went into focus again. How was gravity working here, anyway?

Continuing my thought process: I need to figure out a way to bring my body back to the year 2019, in almost exactly the place and time that I had gone from. But it is far easier to remove energy from a system than to add energy to it unless you remove some energy from that system to replace it with the kind of energy you want to put inside.

And just as I had thought that, something hit me.

I opened my eyes to find myself still falling. But the giant red eye was back again.

Ignoring the eye, I started calculating the energy I would need and where I would get it from.

Oh, but light energy would suffice. But how much?

"Anirudh!" a demonic voice shouted.

I ignored the voice and continued my calculations.

The exact location of the earth relative to where I was and the 'place' I would need to go to in this world to get back to the exact time I needed to get back to was part of my calculations. The location of the earth also depended on time.

"Stop your Insolence!" the voice screamed.

I opened my eyes.

"My insolence? What are you? What do you want from this world?"

Now would be a good time to question this monster. I ran the calculations in the background. It would take a little more time to figure it out, as I had to divert my attention to the big red eyes, but I had all the time in the world.

"We are the Gods of this world."

What?

"An insect-like you wouldn't understand."

"Forget it, what do you want from us?"

"We don't want insignificant beings like you. We want your planet."

"Oh, so you are from another planet."

The being laughed, then spoke, "You have so much to learn. But unfortunately, you wouldn't have the time to. Now die!"

"I can't die here!"

"Of course, but you can die outside your universe!"

A bright light erupted from below. Presumably a portal to…the outside? Wasn't this world already outside the universe?

Was this a bluff? Could I die in this place if I went into the light?

But it didn't matter. My calculations were complete. And not just the calculations, I figured something else as well! All thanks to Mr. Red-eyes opening this portal. Another memory fragment had revealed itself!

I realised that I could make a portal myself! In the same way that the monster opened its portal! A few adjustments to the calculations ('A few' here is an understatement) and done!

A bright flash emerged to my right, like a wormhole. I could see trees through it as if looking through a fishbowl.

Just like the millions of times I had teleported from Ramanujan's world to 1917, all I needed was matter from my body or some kind of substitute energy. But hey Mr Red Eye opened a portal through just energy from brown movements of possibly his universe And the missing memory revealed some of the brown movements in my universe!

And off I went inside.

With a soft thud, I landed on what felt like grass. I stood up and looked around.

I was back on earth. Back inside the three-dimensional world. I might have made some mistakes in the calculations, though, as I had no idea where I was. It seemed to be a forest. What are brown movements, you ask? They are the inherent flow of 'information' throughout the universe that I discovered while analysing the singularities. These brown movements are part of what helped me come back, and how Ramanujan took me from my time into his.

***

"Those beams are very clearly drilling," said Mr Gulpreet, driving the car.

"Drilling for what?" Rohit asked, clueless.

Akriti stared at him, thinking about what answer she should give. "Do you remember Anirudh's dream about the earth exploding?" She said.

"Oh, God!" Rohit exclaimed.

As Shekhar had to go, he had called Mr Gulpreet to meet him midway and take Akriti and Rohit someplace safe. He had been released after RAW realised that Anirudh was not the real threat.

Gruelling images and videos of tanks and helicopters being obliterated could be seen on Akriti's mobile screen as she watched the news. Missiles thrown at the metal tanks had no effect. It was like an impenetrable wall had surrounded the behemoth.

One of the videos showed a beam drilling through a building, making a giant hole in the process. Only certain parts of the building remained and seemed to hang by a thread. But soon a different part of the building started falling to the ground, and like a domino effect, the other parts of it followed suit.

Some videos also showed the movement of large worms through the forest.

"It's terrifying," Rohit said.

Akriti changed the channel. Images of missiles being thrown at the behemoths and the worms could be seen. China had supposedly dropped a hydrogen bomb at one of them.

But the behemoths remained completely unscathed. The worms seemed to be killable, but only after a huge barrage of bombs and bullets.

Everyone fell silent. Only the soft rumbling of the car engine could be heard.

Mr Gulpreet looked at the behemoth visible in the distance from the windscreen and shuddered in fear.

He would have thought more about the creatures, but his phone started ringing.

The call was from Shekhar.

"Hello?" Mr Gulpreet answered the phone.

"Do you remember those EM bursts that were identified by Chandra?"

The phone burst with the sound of the 'breaking news' soundtrack.

"Yes, the ones that were noticed each time a video was uploaded on the Reverter's channel."

The TV spokesperson started talking about how the behemoths had suddenly stopped shooting lasers.

"Yes. A quite big one was noticed the moment Anirudh disappeared along with a strong electromagnetic interference from the location."

"Yes, and?"

"Another big one was identified five minutes ago."

Mr Gulpreet's eyes widened.

"From where?!"

"I have sent you the location."

He frantically searched for the message on his phone. Everyone looked at him with concern and confusion.

"That is…" he said, after finally looking at the message

"Get there immediately! Chandra has started moving as well!" Shekhar said and hung up.

Mr Gulpreet very slowly put his phone down and gulped. He looked at everyone's face, not knowing how to explain.

But there was only one way to say it.

"Anirudh is back."

A chill filled the car.

"Where is he?" Akriti shouted.

"If the location that Shekhar sent is correct, then he is just five minutes away!"

"Drive faster!" Rohit shouted.

The Reverter

XXV

It seemed that I had a few errors in my calculation, but I am glad I didn't end up in space or under the ground. There were lots of things to take into consideration like the rotation of the earth around the sun, its spin on its axis, the rotation of the entire solar system around the black hole of our galaxy and the expansion of the whole universe, along with the brown movements (as Ramanujan likes to call them) of the black hole singularities.

But where was I? I hope I didn't land on another continent. What was this forest I was in?

I stood there for a few minutes just processing what had happened in my 'fight' with the evil being.

Then I heard a faint, but familiar voice I hadn't heard in a very long time. Then another different recognisable voice presented itself, followed by yet another.

And they all seemed to be shouting, "Anirudh! Where are you?"

And soon the voices became closer and closer. And the people to whom these voices belonged became visible in the distance as well. Like sunlight shining through trees, my most beloved humans in all the universe had found me.

Tears filled my eyes as I saw them run towards me.

"Anirudh! Stay right there!" Rohit shouted. He proceeded to punch me. If I hadn't taken a step back, his punch would have knocked me out for sure.

"Where the heck were you?" He shouted as I tried to avoid his barrage of punches.

Then, Akriti came and hugged me. "We were so scared, dumbo!" She said and smiled with her characteristic heartwarming smile.

"I am sorry," I said as tears dropped like a waterfall, "I am back now."

"Where did you go?" Mr Gulpreet asked.

"Yeah, people don't just disappear into thin air!" Rohit shouted.

"I went to a 3-dimensional world just outside the boundaries of our universe through the fourth dimension.

"Huh?" Rohit said, completely perplexed. So were the others.

"What day is it?" I asked.

"It has been about 2 hours since you disappeared. And 1 hour after the curfew started," Rohit said.

"Oh, my calculations really were off. How far are we from the place where I disappeared?"

"About 80 kilometres," said Mr Gulpreet.

"Oops! And a curfew?" I said.

"Yeah, you don't know what has happened, do you? Also, what calculations? A 3-dimensional world outside our universe?" Akriti asked.

"A very, very long story, forget that you need to take me home."

"All right, let's get into the car. We'll talk more while getting there," said Mr Gulpreet.

Then a question popped into my mind as we headed outside the forest, "How did you all know that I would be here?"

Mr Gulpreet replied, "I got a call from Shekhar regarding a strong electromagnetic interference from this location."
"What?" I asked.

"Oh," said Akriti, "Chandra first noticed these electromagnetic fluctuations each time we uploaded a video on our channel. A very large one was noticed when you disappeared and when you came back."
"Oh, Right you mentioned those emfs before. They could be the result of miscalculations and less than a clean exchange of energy. But who is Chandra?" I asked.

Then Rohit looked at me as if I had taken Voldemort's name in the Harry Potter world.
"The guy who tried to kill you! Genius!"
"Oh," I said.

Then something clicked in my brain, and I stopped walking. I was staring ahead with my eyes widened.

It was an Eureka moment.
"What happened?" Akriti asked.
"Electromagnetic forces! Not just that, but the four fundamental forces of nature! They have been right there for 2000 years in my brain as I played with the data from the singularity! And if electromagnetic fluctuations were noticed each time we made a huge change, then that means a significant change was produced in the universal time crystal! And for that change to happen…"
"2000 years?!" Akriti said.

I continued, "You see, I have gained only a macro level of control over the universe as I figured out how to turn back spacetime to a previous state during my encounter with the singularity. But it was too much data to process! So my brain shut the memories after I managed to turn back the whole universe. Meanwhile, my brain developed to process the information better. I only understood partly how I turned it back during the 2000 years of my meditation-induced exploration. But now I understand! It is similar to the usage of brown movements in Ramanujan's method of interdimensional travel after incorporating my theory of universal time crystals into the loop-quantum-gravity theory! Brown movements are linking the spin network with 4th-dimensional time vectors! This allows me to use the quantum electrodynamic forces to create a time-crystal loop! And then I can revert this loop, reverting the brown movements, in turn reverting the whole universe itself back in time! Thanks to Chandra, I have made tremendous progress!"

"What?!" said Rohit.

"Now, I only need to do this on the micro-scale! In a space less than a Planck length! To test it out. And then I can scale up from there and basically…"

"Anirudh, are you ok?" Akriti asked,

Everyone was looking at me in confusion while I was gleefully smiling except for Mr Gulrpreet, who appeared to be in deep thought.

"Anirudh, you need to tell me about these brown movements. Can they be described using ashtekar variables?"

"Maybe, but let's talk about this later. Get me home. There is something I must experiment with there."

"Oh no, we can't take you back home!" He said.

"Why?"

"Chandra is after you! We must take you somewhere far away from here!"

I could hear the sound of helicopters approaching from far away. I could also sense something big coming towards us.

Mr Gulpreet immediately got a call. It was from Shekhar. He put the phone on speaker.

"Hello, Shekhar! We have found Anirudh! You are on speaker!"

"Anirudh run! Chandra Is…" The phone then abruptly cut and a large boom was heard behind us.

We could see smoke rising. Birds flew up from the trees around us and flew frantically all around. I could no longer detect the presence of the helicopter. But the big thing was there.

A roar erupted from the direction of the smoke.

"Let's get out of here!" I screamed. And we started running towards the road where the car was parked.

After a few seconds, we reached the street. Thanks to the curfew, there was no one on the road except for Mr Gulpreet's car. The car was a little farther to the left, but we needed to hurry, as I could still sense the big thing.

The ground had started to rumble and you could also see the trees falling one after the other. It was only after Mr Gulpreet had started the car that the final set of trees fell, revealing a gigantic worm.

"Shit! Drive!" Rohit shouted.

Mr Gulpreet slammed the gas pedal, and the car lunged forward. The worm followed.

The worm was slow, but more worms were emerging from the forest. The car sped ahead, leaving the worms behind, but they just wouldn't stop coming out of the forest!

It would have been fine as long as they were behind us, but then they started to pop from in front of us.

"Not again!" Akriti shrieked.

"Hold on Kids!" Mr Gulpreet shouted.

"The road is blocked!" Rohit screamed. There were too many worms coming towards us from the front and the back. To make matters worse, I could feel the trees falling from our right and left.

We were being surrounded.

Then I heard jets flying above us. Light orange light flashed onto us as loud booms sounded all around us.

The fighter jets were fighting the worms.

A worm lay ahead on fire and blocked the road.

"Ok now really hold on to something. I am going to apply the brakes.

"No! Keep going!" I said.

"What?" Akriti shouted.

"Just trust me!"

It was simply the manipulation of energy. Thanks to Ramanujan, I got used to and better at the calculations required. And I just had some more practice when I came back to 2019 and I just had that Eureka moment. It was all coming together.

So with a bright flash which engulfed the car, in an instant the battleground had changed into the city of Mumbai.

Mr Gulpreet immediately pulled over to the side of the road and applied the brakes.

After the car stopped, he turned around to face me and said, "What in God's good name was that?"

Rohit and Akriti were just as perplexed and were staring at me with shocked faces.

"Teleportation!" I replied, smiling gleefully.

We were now near the entrance of Mira Road, the northernmost western suburb of Mumbai, just before Vasai-Virar. I could see a few residential buildings outside the car. And I could also see the behemoths as shown by the evil entity in that 4th-dimensional world, except that they weren't shooting lasers.

The entity was not lying. It sought to destroy our planet for whatever reason. But that didn't scare me at all.

What scared me was the fact that I could sense an evil aura around us. I don't know why, but I sensed something bad was about to happen.

"Let's get out of the car for a moment," I said as the car started to feel a little suffocating.

"Yeah, I could use a little fresh air," said Akriti.

So we got out of the car and all of us took deep breaths. No one said anything to each other. 2301 years of meditation and I still felt uneasy for some reason.

And soon my reason for uneasiness would reveal itself.

Yes, Chandra was here.

A bright flash erupted ahead in the middle of the street.

And there he was, standing, with a sinister smile.

"But he was supposed to be in Alibagh! How did he get here so fast?!" Akriti shouted.

"The same way we got here."

"Alas! We meet again human." He said in an almost robotic voice.

The fear on Akriti's face was telling.

"You cannot kill me! Not while I am in my universe!" I shouted.

"Oh, but I can kill him!" He shouted.

Blood rained down on me from my left as I saw Rohit Impaled on a very sharp meat-like stick protruding from the ground.

"No!" I shouted.

The stick went back into the ground, making Rohit fall to the ground with a disheartening smack.

Akriti uttered a guttural shriek.

I stood there frozen. But anger seethed through my blood. How could this monster do this? How could he kill my best friend? Memories of us spending time together came to my mind. All those happy times were now down the drain.

But then it hit me. I knew what I had to do. The brown movements flowing through the time crystal were in my control through the 4th dimension and the quantum loops. I needed to repeat the teleportation process at the Planck length and that should do the trick.

I am the reverter, and I shall revert the universe. Rohit had not died. I can't let him.

You could say it happened in a millisecond, or it took a million years. But time is arbitrary when you are trying to save your friend.

It was time to test my theory and my godly enhanced senses.

And thus, with a few billion steps, I turned back the universe to about a minute before Rohit was killed.

***

A bright flash erupted ahead in the middle of the street.

And there he was, standing, with a sinister smile.

I had successfully reverted the universe. I turned left to see Rohit alive and well.

Chandra's smile immediately turned into a frown.

"What did you do?!" he screamed.

Now, it was my turn to smile.

"You can kill whoever you want, and I can keep reverting the state of the universe. We have reached a stalemate."

"For how long!? You cannot possibly keep reverting the universe!"

"Oh, I can do this all day."
"Oh, can you now?"
In the blink of an eye, the world around me changed again. I was back in the place of my visions. A red sky of gushing flesh with red waterfalls in the sky. A scorched earth with random collapsed buildings on fire.

But in this place, it was only me and an enormous machine in front of me. A being made entirely of metal…that seemed flesh-like it was dripping blood from all over and appeared somewhat like a Racoon with a giant head and red eyes.

This was my world. Rather, this was supposed to be my world. Just like Ramanujan's.

The Racoon moved its arm towards me to try to smash me. But what would that do?

I teleported to escape it.

It attacked again.

I teleported again.

"What are you trying to achieve?" I asked, "You can't kill me here!"
"I don't need to."

Oh, no, not this again. I immediately tried to teleport myself back to 2019. But for some reason, I couldn't.
"What have you done?" I screamed.
It attacked me again. I teleported again. Teleportation had become almost automatic now, yet I couldn't get out of this outer world.
All of a sudden, a bright flash erupted above the monster and huge swords fell onto it.
"But you can get inside it!" said a voice I had come to love. It was Ramanajun.
"Oh, my Goodness!" I screamed in delight.

The swords had penetrated the monster. They didn't kill it, but it was definitely injured. It fell with a loud thud and a metallic clank. It was trying to get up, but struggled to get the swords out of the way.

"It's using the last of its energy to counter any form of energy flowing out of this world," said Sir Ramanujan, who had appeared to my left.

"But why?"

The monster was almost on its feet now.

"Because Chandra and the behemoths are there. They are quite possibly manifestations of some other source of energy from his world. Or maybe this monster in front of us is. Another reason could be that you can't revert the universe without being inside it. Ok, that is definitely it."

The monster had figured it out and was now on its feet. It removed the sword out of its chest and feet and began charging at us with the sword in hand.

"What do we do?"

"Watch and learn."

A bright flash emanated from above us and more swords came and started to attack the monster. But the monster still lunged forward.

"Uh, swords are cool but.."

The monster dashed forward and attacked me. I fell to the ground and tried to dodge it.

It came for another slash, and I rolled to avoid it. But it immediately came for another slash. But before it could hit me, I teleported behind the monster.

I also realised how Ramanujan was conjuring the swords. He simply converted that matter around us into whatever he wanted.

The monster now attacked Ramanujan, but he dodged it.

"Anirudh! This thing has very limited energy left from its world! This is why it wants the earth."

I understood what he was trying to say. Because of the high concentration of living beings on Earth, many worlds like this current world have been created and thus there would be more energy. This creature simply wants to devour that energy.

"Then we must drain all of its energy!"

I focused on the air around us and converted it into discrete and highly compressed beams with high energy.

Off went the laser beams onto the monster.

"Ha!" Shouted Ramanujan.

The monster roared. It then turned back and started attacking me again.

But Ramanujan attacked it again. It roared and turned to attack Ramanujan. But then I attacked again.

"It's working!" I shouted.
"Keep attacking! It's losing any energy that it has!" He shouted.
Then both Ramanujan and I started attacking it repeatedly.

And the Mighty Raccoon had been slain.

The world around us was becoming dark, as if all light was being taken away from the world except for the monster, Ramanujan, and me. I started to feel weightless.

And with a bright flash, the monster disappeared.

I felt very serene. It felt like a huge weight had been lifted from my back or as if my nose had been blocked for months and I could finally breathe properly.
"Remarkable!" said Ramanujan as he came towards me with his arms stretched wide. I opened my arms and hugged him.
"Alright, I bet you can see more of what is happening now in the Universe. You need to sever any remaining links of the evil being. And you still need to be aware of Chandra."
"I will! See you soon!"
"Sense the world around you!"
And with that, I quickly teleported back to 2019.

The Finishing Blow

XXVI

I was back in 2019. Mr Gulpreet was driving the car. Rohit was sitting in the front seat while my head rested on a pillow over Akriti's lap. I immediately got up.

"Oh, you're awake!" Akriti screamed.

"Wooh!" Rohit and Mr Gupta cheered.

"You won't believe the kind of fight I just came from."

"What? Bro, you and Chandra just collapsed all of a sudden. We picked you up and ran," Rohit said.

"Oh, ok…Where are we?"

"Almost home." Mr Gulpreet said

A sharp, pulsating sound announced itself without warning.

"The behemoths are back online," Akriti said.

Out of nowhere, something hit the roof of the car with a bang. Mr Gulpreet immediately stopped the car.

Bang!

A bullet pierced through the roof. Everyone screamed and got out of the car.

And Chandra was standing right at the top. He was pointing his gun at us.

"Stop you four!" He shouted. We stopped running. I could just teleport the bullet if he shot, but I wanted to knock some sense into Chandra.

"Chandra, whatever the being has told you is wrong! Put the gun down!" I said.

"He is our messiah!"

"Dude, look around you!" I pointed at the behemoths. "Do you seriously believe he wants to save us?"

"Shut up! You can fool your friends, but you can't fool me! These things are *your* puppets!"

He was far too gone to talk about it. I immediately teleported behind him and pushed him down the car.

He almost fell, but then teleported behind me and pushed me down. I fell with a loud thud!

"You think I can't do that?" he shouted. I should have thought about it…

Suddenly a bullet shot sounded, and a bullet vaporized to the right of Chandra.

"Run!" said Shekhar. I don't know where he came from, but impeccable timing!

"Oh, no you don't." Chandra immediately teleported in front of Shekhar and knocked him out with a punch in an instant.

I tried sensing the surrounding matter just as I would in the higher dimension, and it worked. With some help from the higher dimension, I could now freely manipulate matter in this universe and my outer world!

Before Chandra could do anything about it, I immediately threw him up with a bolt of rocks that shot up from the ground.

But Chandra didn't fall. He teleported again to hit me but I realised it and hit him with a car.

Chandra had finally fallen to the ground and didn't look like he would get up soon.

"Whoa!" Rohit exclaimed.

"Quickly let's go!" I screamed.

We took the opportunity and got into our car. Mr Gulpreet immediately drove towards my house, visible a few 100 metres ahead.

I tried analysing the behemoths as well.

"The behemoths have black holes in their centres."

"Why? And how was this evil being able to bring them into our world? Through the 4th dimension?" Akriti asked.

"Let me think," I said.

On further inspection, I realised, "There is another spin network interfering with the brown movements of these black holes!"

"Speak English please," Rohit said.

"This means that there was another universe! A Multiverse indeed exists! So this being wasn't just drawing power from its outer world, but a whole other universe! I imagine bringing these behemoths here would have taken quite some amount of energy. These Behemoths not only had black holes inside, but they were constantly drawing energy from them."

"Can you stop them?" Mr Gulpreet asked.

"Yes! With my experience with brown movements. And thanks to me claiming back my outer world, I could block them on a macro level! That should stop the evil being!"

That was it!

All I had to do was to block the other universe's brown movements inside this universe!

And I did! It took some time as I had to have my fourth-dimensional self go and sever those connections, but I did it!

The behemoths immediately disappeared with a bright flash! The world appeared like it was full of gigantic fireflies. A weird pulsating could be heard as well and then poof! The Behemoths were gone.

I could imagine people coming out of their homes around the world gaping in awe as to where the metallic beasts went. The military and navy men and women taking their caps off and just stared stupefied at the brilliant sight.

"Oh my God they're gone!" Exclaimed Mr Gulpreet.

"Yes!" Rohit shouted.

"Amazing!" Akriti said.

But then I heard a motorcycle behind us.

It was Chandra.

But I had cut off the brown movements! How was he still following us?

He was at some distance, but it wouldn't take long to catch up to us.

"Drive faster!" Akriti shouted.

"We have almost reached! Hold on!" Mr Gulpreet said as he pumped the gas.

And we had indeed reached. Fortunately, the gate was already open.

Chandra was catching up.

"Everybody out of the car now!"

"Ok, but where do we go?" asked Mr Gulpreet.

"The entity is completely blind right now, as I have cut off the brown movements of his universe inside ours. I don't know why Chandra is still on our tail."

"Good! Then let's split up Rohit, Anirudh and I will go to Anirudh's house and you go to that building, and get help," Akriti said, pointing out to the A-wing of our complex.

"But!" He said.

"Good plan, let's go! He is probably very weak now! Now let's go!" I interjected.

We immediately got out and started running.

The A-wing was far closer than where we had to go.

The sound of the bike was getting closer, and soon Chandra had entered the complex.

"Faster!" Rohit shouted.

Mr Gulpreet was already inside the building, but my wing was a little farther.

Unfortunately, Chandra had already seen us and was chasing us on foot.

We ran as fast as we could, but Chandra was getting closer.

We finally reached the building and ran inside. But the moment I stepped inside the building, everything turned completely white.

It was the same white which I had found myself after that earthquake. The same white that had pushed me into Akriti's dream.

And at that instant, the final memory fragment of my encounter with the singularity had unlocked.

I could finally see it all! The theory of everything was complete! My mind was racing! It all made sense!

And this white world. This benevolent entity was there with me when I first encountered the singularity!

It was the singularity! It was a living being born out of the sheer chaos of energy!

I stood in awe, staring at the bright world. A singular metallic ball lay in front of me. It gave out an ethereal glow. This was it.

A bright flash erupted to my left.
"You've done it!" Said Mr Ramanujan.
"I indeed have!"

***

Chandra thought to himself, "What have I been doing?"

He was chasing the reverter with all his might. He had killed so many people.

But why?

Was it because of those dreams he had been having?

Why had he been so demented? What had taken over him? Why was he so hell-bent on capturing the reverter that he killed his own friend? Why did his memory seem so fuzzy?

He then remembered his family, his daughter. How had he neglected everyone so much?

These thoughts tormented him as he ran towards the three children running towards the building.

He looked around to see a bunch of headless people in camouflage with guns. It horrified him.

The kids reached the building, and he was just a few meters away.

"These kids could answer my questions. I need to reach them. I need to ask them for help. They must know something!" He thought.

"Wait!" He shouted.

But the kids didn't hear him.

He once again gave it his all and started running with all his might. He entered the building and heard hurried footsteps coming from the staircase on the right.

"Hey! Stop!" He screamed.

He started running up the spiralling stairs. He could see the kids going up the seemingly endless serpent of stairs.

He called out to them, his voice echoing off the walls, which now made him feel claustrophobic.

But they didn't listen.

His legs were starting to feel heavy; each step was now requiring tremendous effort. He could feel a dull ache in his chest, as he was going out of breath.

The air was growing colder. He could hear the faint whisper of the wind through the windows around the stairs.

The sun was setting down as well. But the kids continued upwards.

He had gotten closer to them.

Despite the pain he felt, he had gained on them.

"Stop! Please!" He shouted.

The soldiers behind him had started to fall one by one. But he didn't care. The kids were now almost within reach.

The kids gave him a fearful grin.

Except for one.

That one kid smiled at him as if saying that it was alright.

His smile made him feel a bit relaxed. It felt like someone who he had committed grave atrocities against had forgiven him.

But he had to talk to them.

There was this door on each floor of the staircase. And the kids went to it on the next floor.

The door was opened; the kids went through, and the door was shut.

Chandra also went towards it and opened it.

But what he saw defied all logic and expectation. He had anticipated the familiar sight of walls and doors typical of an apartment complex.

Instead, he found a vast ground leading to a wall, behind which were tall residential buildings. To his right was another stretch of land, which ended with an entrance to a building.
He followed the building as he turned around to see himself standing at the entrance of the very building he had just entered.
"How am I on the ground floor?" he thought to himself.

Confused and dejected, he sat on the ground, taking his breath and staring at the entrance of the building to his right.
It was over.

Epilogue

Akriti woke up on her bed and stretched. She stared straight ahead, confused.

"Where am I?" she asked herself.

She looked around and realised that this was her room. She then picked up her phone from the side table and pressed the power button to see the time.

The lock screen read, '5:23 PM, Friday, 5th April 2019. You have 12 unread notifications.'

"5th April?!" Akriti screamed. "Was everything just a dream?"

Suddenly, her phone started ringing.

It was Rohit. Her eyes widened, and she quickly accepted the call.

"Hello? Rohit? What is going on? Where is Anirudh?"

"Come to the Terrace of Anirudh's building. A-Wing that is."

"Weren't we just there?"

"Yeah, I know. Just come to the terrace. Anirudh is here."

"Coming!"

She quickly cut the call and ran outside. She almost forgot to wear her sandals.

And soon she reached the terrace. She saw me standing beside Rohit, leaning against the railing. We turned back to face her as she entered the terrace,

"Come here", I said calmly, smiling.

She came and stood to my left, leaning against the railing.

"I can't believe that you kept our memories," Rohit said.

We were looking at the Mumbai city from the terrace of my apartment building. The sun setting cast a golden glow on the city. All felt calm.

"Akriti wouldn't be a friend anymore and you, Rohit, would have gone and died in the war," I said.

"Was that evil entity not a cause for the war?" Rohit asked.

"No, it is still very much a human creation. The Entity just wanted to devour our universe. I just reverted the universe to ensure a normal flow of time."

"So, this doesn't mean the war won't happen," Akriti stated.

"Yes, there is still more work to be done. Preventing the pandemic is also one of them."

"Should we still make a YouTube channel?" She asked.

"The Reverter? No. That won't really work. It didn't the last time."

"So, how will you change everything?" Rohit asked.

"By subtly influencing everyone's mind. I don't have complete control over everything in this universe. I still have to conserve energy. But I can still plant ideas into people's minds. I can influence people's dreams. As all living things have their higher dimensional counterparts."

"Is that how you entered my dream?" Akriti asked.

"Yes, sort of."

"Won't it be a lot of work?" Rohit asked.

"Yes, but I will have some help. But that isn't the issue. There are more people like me. I know they are here, and I know that they are aware of my existence."

"Who are these people?" Akriti asked.

"Ordinary people like me, people from scientific backgrounds like Sir Ramanujan, and interestingly, most of the religious figures we know about in our religious texts."

"Woah, like Jesus?" Rohit asked.

"Lord Rama? Prophet Mohammad? The Buddha?" Akriti asked,
"Yes, although I am not sure if I can reach them. They all had their eras of influence."
"Wow, so all gods exist? I better pray every day," Rohit chuckled.
I smiled and said, "Sure, but they can only hear you. Don't expect them to just grant your wishes, although even thinking about it is astounding."
"This is exciting and terrifying!" Rohit exclaimed. "I can't quite understand what I am feeling. All Gods exist! All religions are right!"
"Yes and no, but I won't complicate it further."

Akriti was staring at the horizon. After a while, she spoke, "This is unbelievable. I can't believe everything that happened. It feels like a distant dream."
"If that is what you want it to be…"

Akriti immediately turned to me and said, "There is so much suffering in this world. Can't you just end it? Hunger, poverty, all the crimes and all the pain the people suffer."
"This is a long conversation I had with Sir Ramanujan. I have to prevent the war as well, But I still need to preserve the human will. All Gods before me have tried to end suffering in their own way, but it is the very human nature that prevents us. And as I said, any significant change requires lots of energy. I may have found a loophole that helps me revert the universe at will though, but again, it is not so easy. The religions were created by the gods for this very reason. Because influencing people that way is easier."
Akriti stared ahead. So did Rohit. We were all looking at the world.
"Oh my God!" Rohit exclaimed.
"What happened?" Akriti asked.
"I will have to write all my notes again!" He exclaimed.
We all started laughing.
"Don't worry, I'll help you with that," I said with a wink.

"Sure buddy, sure. Bro saved the whole universe but forgot about school work."

And we continued talking with each other. It was lovely. All very lovely.

I looked at the clear golden-orange sky. And thanked the good entity. I still didn't understand what exactly it was. There was a lot that I needed to understand. But I was glad that it existed and granted me its presence. Because it was the true nature of the world.

But if it was gone, then the universe would be vulnerable to attacks from the others, just like the entity that controlled the behemoths did.

An alliance of all the people like me was now necessary.

My thoughts were suddenly interrupted by the sound of a telephone ringing.

I turned around to see an old, black, rotary dial phone placed on a wooden stool.

The phone kept ringing.

"What happened?" Akriti asked as she noticed me turn around. Rohit turned around as well.

"Was this here before?" I asked.

"What was here before?" Rohit asked.

"The telephone," I said, pointing at it.

The telephone was still ringing.

"I don't see any telephone, Anirudh," Akriti said.

"I don't either," Rohit said

The telephone stopped ringing.

I went towards it and picked it up. I turned it all around to see if it was real. It was definitely real.

I placed it back on the stool, and it started ringing again.

I picked up the receiver and placed it against my ear.

"How in the bloody world is this possible?" said the voice on the phone.

Acknowledgements

What an incredible journey this has been! Writing "The Reverter" has been an absolute dream come true, and I am immensely grateful to everyone who helped me along the way and provided invaluable feedback.

Firstly, I want to express my deepest gratitude to Aman and Aditya. Without their presence, encouragement, and insightful feedback, this book would never have come to fruition. Aditya, thank you for introducing me to the concept of story structures and for being the very first person to read the initial chapters of my book. Your guidance was instrumental in shaping the foundation of this story. Aman, your unwavering support as I wrote each chapter, your meticulous editing, and your creative ideas were indispensable. It is thanks to you that "The Reverter" is as polished and readable as it is today.

I would also like to extend my heartfelt thanks to Abhinaya, who was there during the book's early stages and provided invaluable feedback that helped steer the story in the right direction. Your insights were incredibly helpful and greatly appreciated.

To all the beta readers, especially Tarun, I owe a tremendous debt of gratitude. Tarun, your keen eye for detail helped identify continuity errors and provided deeper insights into the chapters, making the story more cohesive and engaging. I am also grateful to the members of the Indian Writers Discord server, who took the time to read the book and offered specific and constructive feedback.

Your collective input has been invaluable in refining the narrative and enhancing the overall quality of the book.

A special thank you to my parents, whose unwavering support and encouragement over the past two years have been a source of strength and motivation. Your belief in my dream kept me going through the challenges and triumphs of this writing journey.

I also want to acknowledge all my English teachers, who have played a significant role in building my confidence as a writer. Your lessons and encouragement have been fundamental in helping me develop my writing skills and pursue my passion for storytelling.

To everyone who has been a part of this journey, whether through direct involvement or by offering a word of encouragement, thank you from the bottom of my heart. "The Reverter" is not just a product of my imagination and effort but also a testament to the support and contributions of an incredible community of friends, family, and mentors.

Thank you all for being a part of this unforgettable journey.

Note To Reader

Thank you for reading The Reverter! This was my first novel, and I am absolutely delighted that you read my book!

If you liked it, spread the word! Go tell your friends, your colleagues, your parents about how much of a fun read this was! Post about on social media! Leave a review!

And if you want to hear more from me:

You can subscribe to my newsletter on achintyanigam-writes.carrd.co

You can follow me on X (Formerly known as twitter): @achintyawrites

You can follow me on Instagram: @achintya_nigam

Why did I write this novel?

Because I felt that there was a need of a good sci-fi story out there set in India. And also because I had a fun idea. And why not write your own novel?

Although this book is still more general, I would be writing things that go more in depth into the Indian culture.

So thank you so much for reading my first novel!

There is more to come!

Anirudh will Return!

Note To Reader

www.ingramcontent.com/pod-product-compliance
Lightning Source LLC
LaVergne TN
LVHW012046160826
845678LV00014B/2713

* 9 7 8 9 3 3 4 0 9 1 4 4 1 *